# Born

To Carol

# Born

Ryan Sam Turner

Thanks for the support

First published in 2021
by Balladeer Books Limited

Printed and bound by CPI Group (UK) Ltd, Croydon, CR0 4YY



A CIP record for this book is available from the British Library.

ISBN: 978-0-9562570-4-8

For my family

# baby james

I remember the phone call. It was the kind of call that you dread, the kind that will stay with you forever. It was the unimaginable, the unforgettable. It was life-changing. I was in the middle of teaching a lesson when I felt my mobile phone vibrating in my trouser pocket. Without hesitation I left the classroom to answer the call. It was Sarah, crying hysterically. When she spoke, she sounded broken, her voice almost inaudible. Eventually she babbled it out. Something was wrong with the baby, our baby, our son-to-be, our precious, precious James.

'Mark, she can't find anything.'

'Who can't?'

'The midwife. She said there's nothing there.'

'What do you mean? What can't she find?'

'A heartbeat ... she can't find a heartbeat.'

Sarah just about managed to finish the sentence before breaking down completely. I could hear her bubbling down the phone line.

'Sarah, listen to me: it'll be fine. Everything will be okay.'

'How – how will it?' she stuttered.

'Well, maybe there's something wrong with the tests, or maybe the equipment they're using is faulty. I mean, you've read the stories in the news, the crazy stories of major misdiagnosis. Maybe they've got it completely wrong and made a mistake; an honest mistake.'

I spoke in a hopeful tone though I was struggling to convince myself, let alone her. I was clinging to straws, desperately.

'Do you think – do you think he could be okay?'

She sounded more positive, tears slowly retreating, voice clearer.

'It's possible. So, what happens now?' I asked.

'I'm on my way to the hospital for a second check, a second opinion.'

'Well, I'll meet you there. I'll leave right now.'

'Please do. I need you.'

'No problem. I'll just get my things together and come straight away.'

'Thank you.'

'And listen – don't worry, not yet.'

When the call ended, I felt an overwhelming sensation of fear, something I'd never experienced before. My face drained of colour, leaving it a pale shade of pastel grey, and my stomach was tied in knots and locked with bolts. I could sense the approach of loss already.

Though I'd promised to join Sarah as soon as I could, I found it almost impossible to drag my leaden feet back into the classroom. When I did manage that task, the pupils were all chattering amongst themselves, but most fell silent as they watched me stumble back to my desk. I opened the drawer, took out my car keys and wallet, and walked straight out without an explanation. I didn't bother telling any of the other teachers where I was going, not even the rector.

As it was November, shimmering ice and frost coated most of the pathways. I ran hurriedly to the car park, almost losing my footing a number of times on the glacial terrain. Despite the conditions underfoot I refused to slow my pace, and somehow made it to the car unscathed.

In my car – a newly purchased family saloon – I began the nerve-jangling drive to the Royal Infirmary, in the south-east of the city; the opposite side of Edinburgh. I wanted to get there as quickly as possible, so I could be by my wife's side, so I could hold her hand and support her, but for most of the way I was followed by a police car and couldn't go anywhere over the speed limit. When they eventually left my tail I put the accelerator pedal to the floor and got there within forty-five minutes, an achievement given the circumstances.

At the hospital, my newfound streak of bad luck continued. The car park was heaving; it looked practically full. Ten infuriating minutes later I found a space, although it was one of those farthest away from the hospital complex. I was in such a rush to get to Sarah that I had the car door open and one foot on the ground before I'd even turned the engine off. I sprinted for the main entrance, dodging a number of oncoming cars and ambulances. Slowing my speed a little, I power-walked through the automatic doors and into the hospital.

The brightness of the lights inside made my eyes water. I had to stand still and let them grow used to the glare. As my blurred eyesight cleared, I became aware of another reminder of where I was. My nose began to twitch under a familiar, unwelcome onslaught. You know exactly what I mean: it was the stench of death, defeat, despair, overlaid but not drowned out by powerful cleaning products.

There was a long line of people queuing at reception but I didn't have it in me to wait. I pushed my way to the front and was on the receiving end of some harsh comments from those that had at least some remnants of patience. Despite my queue-jumping and general lack of manners, the receptionist could sense the urgency of my request and gave me directions to the maternity ward.

Although her directions didn't sound all that hard to follow, I struggled to do just that, and had to ask for another set from a young nurse as I rushed aimlessly through the long, winding, never-ending labyrinth of white-walled corridors. Not long after that, I managed to find my way to the maternity ward, and that's where I found Sarah.

Through a small square window in a closed door I could see her lying in a bed, with her head hiding in her hands. With that view, I knew that the worst had been confirmed; that it really was true, it really was over.

I opened the door and walked in with slow, tentative steps. A nurse was standing next to the bed – I assumed that she was the midwife – holding out a box of tissues for Sarah. The first thing I did was ask her whether it was true. I wasn't going to accept it fully until I'd heard it officially. In a quiet, regretful voice, she confirmed the fact that James's heart had stopped beating, that it had probably been still for several days, and that he was gone. She told us that she'd give us a while to talk things over. Before she left the room, she handed me the box of tissues, which I placed on the bed. The door closed behind her, leaving the two of us overshadowed by our dark cloud of grief. Sarah was now sitting up, but her head was still stuck firmly in her own grasp. Crouching over the bed, I held her awkwardly, kissing the top of her head. Tears rolled down my face, landing on her auburn hair. I stood like that for a while until eventually she wrapped her arms around me. Sorrow and pain made her familiar face almost unrecognisable.

'I'm so sorry,' she said in a shaky voice.

Her lips trembled, as if she was freezing from the cold outside.

'It's not your fault,' I replied in an equally broken and worn-out tone.

'I should have known something was wrong with him. You heard the midwife ... he's probably been dead for days.'

'Don't be silly. There's no way you could have known.'

I stroked her face. She turned her head away.

'Of course I could have. I should have checked his movements more. I should have checked that he was still active, and maybe if I had, he would still be alive. What have I done?'

'It's not your fault,' I told her again, but she didn't want my sympathy.

She let go of me and raised her hands to her face once more, then higher to her head. She ran her fingers through her hair and began pulling hard on her auburn locks.

'I've let you down. I've let everyone down.'

I grabbed her hands with a caring force to release the tight grip she had on her hair.

'I can understand why you feel like this, but I swear you've done nothing wrong. I know you're feeling awful just now, but it will pass eventually. You couldn't have done anything more than you have. You've been amazing.'

'I've lost a child, Mark! He would have been born in two weeks!' she said in a slightly raised voice while pushing my hands away.

'And I've lost one too. I'm just as upset as you are, but you can't go blaming yourself for something that's beyond your control. This isn't your fault. It's the fault of life itself. These things happen. They happen to lots of people. They happen on a daily basis. You need to listen to me – it's not your fault.'

Once again I held her, and kissed her on the lips before speaking.

'I love you,' I said, expecting to hear the same in return. But there was no return. Sarah was crying harder now and was too upset to say anything. That was the reason for the silence, or at least I hoped that it was.

Neither of us could find another word to say. I sat down on the uncomfortable pretend-leather-covered chair next to her bed. It was the kind of chair you only find in hospitals and old people's homes; the easy-clean, faintly smelly kind that makes your back ache after five minutes. It was solid and unyielding. It felt like it was made from stone. We sat in silence, trying to take in what had happened, trying to understand just what exactly the day had thrown at us.

After a while the midwife re-entered the room with a wad of pamphlets in her hand. Before she could say anything to us, I asked her what we were supposed to do now. What was normal after something like this? What would happen to our baby? She pulled over another horrible chair, sat down and explained things. She outlined several options that were all equally grim and distressing to listen to, but she told us that the safest option, and the most common one, was a natural delivery. I didn't know much about stillbirths. To be truthful, I'd never considered the subject. Her suggestion caught me off guard.

'Are you sure that's right?' I asked, shocked.

She nodded her head and proceeded to reel off a list of reasons in favour of a natural delivery, following that up with a more extensive list of alternatives she didn't feel able to recommend. Her suggestions seemed biased to me, completely one-sided, but she knew best, I reasoned. She was the only one in the room with any experience of this situation.

Either way, the choice wasn't mine to make, and I was glad of that. I asked Sarah which option she preferred, seeing as it was her body and ultimately her choice, but she didn't care whatsoever. She was numb and distant, her teary eyes glazed over and blank. When pressed she decided to go with the midwife's recommendation, and that was that. That huge decision was made without a second thought. The midwife didn't ask twice; nor did she offer further reassurance. She ticked a box and left the room, off to make the necessary arrangements for us.

The earliest appointment that the hospital could give us was in three days' time. That's how long we'd be forced to wait for the birth of our dead son. I challenged the timescale that the midwife quoted. To me, making us wait so long seemed cruel. I didn't want Sarah to endure another second of what she was going through, let alone another three days of it; but we were told firmly that this was the earliest possible time that the delivery could be arranged. We had to try to accept it and move on; there was no argument to be had.

Before we left, the midwife handed me the leaflets she'd been holding in readiness. The paper was warm and filmed with moisture from her sweaty palm. As I took them from her, she put her hand on my shoulder and pulled me close. Her head moved to the side of mine. I could feel her breath fanning my ear as she whispered: 'You'll need to keep a close watch on Sarah. You'll really need to look after her. She'll be very fragile right now. You need to be her ark. You need to weather the storm.'

I nodded and told her that I would. Satisfied with my response, she took her hand off my shoulder and left. We were now ready to leave too, ready to escape. I gripped Sarah's hand tightly and we left the hospital together, in pieces.

The sky had turned black but for a bright full moon and the handful of glistening stars that hung around it. The temperature had plummeted to well below freezing. We both began to shiver uncontrollably. The darkness and the cold summed up the whole mood of that devastating day.

When I put my parking ticket in the meter, I was charged £7. We'd just lost a child but the money-making machine ground on. What a fucking ridiculous thing! On the drive home I ranted about it; about how people died in that hospital every day and their relatives had to pay for the privilege of seeing them one final time. I really couldn't get my head around it. I couldn't find any justification.

Sarah sat and pretended to listen, but I could tell that my diatribe was going in one ear and out the other. She didn't speak. For most of the journey home, she stared out of the passenger-seat window while a steady flow of tears trickled down her cheeks and travelled all the way down to her neck. Every now and again she'd wipe the tears away with the sleeve of her grey merino wool cardigan, dampening it to black.

Whenever we got stuck at a red light or in slow-moving traffic, I would slide my left hand across from the gear stick and place it on her shoulder. She didn't flinch or even acknowledge me, but sat slumped in her seat, abandoned to despair.

It was just after 7 p.m. when we left the hospital. In the heavy traffic, it took us over an hour and a half to get back to our flat in Corstorphine. It felt like days. It was frustrating, mentally exhausting. When we arrived, I got out of the car first and opened the door for Sarah. I helped her out and held her hand as we walked through the main door of the building and up the winding stairs that led to our third-floor flat. As Sarah was so far gone in her pregnancy, it took her a while to climb the steps. I followed close behind, helping her with each one, my hands supporting her back.

On our landing, I opened the front door and let her enter first. She walked straight into the bedroom and collapsed on the bed in a heap, curling up into a ball. She began crying softly.

'Are you okay?'

Immediately, I regretted asking such an unintelligent question. Of course she wasn't okay. She'd spent the majority of the last year in joyous expectation, carrying a child, bonding with it, having it grow inside her, and now she'd never get to see it live.

'That's a really fucking stupid question!' she said.

'I know. I just realised what I said. I'm so sorry.'

'So you should be.'

The conversation stalled. I stood there, hopelessly staring at her, unsure of what to do or say.

'Do you want to rest just now?' I asked, breaking the tense intermission.

'Yes, please. I'm drained.'

'Do you need anything? Would you like me to get you anything, something to eat or drink maybe?'

'No, thanks. I couldn't stomach anything.'

'Are you sure?'

'Yes, I'm sure.'

'Okay, I'll leave you alone for a while to rest, but if there's anything you want, anything you need, just shout on me. I'll be in the living room.'

I was walking out when Sarah spoke up again.

'Wait! What happens now? What about our families? What about my parents and my sister ... and what about your parents? What are we going to tell them? I don't think I can speak to anyone. I don't think I can tell anyone what's happened.'

'That's okay. I'll sort all that out. You don't need to worry about anything. Just get some rest.'

'They're all going to hate me, aren't they? They're all going to be ashamed of me.'

'No one's going to hate you. You've done everything right. You need to stop blaming yourself for this, and you've got to do it right now!'

'I don't know if I can.'

'Well, you need to try. You need to be strong.'

'I know,' she said in a whisper. Her eyes closed and she turned away from me.

'Right, I'm going to leave you now. Try and get some rest.'

I left the door ajar so I could hear if Sarah shouted for anything. In the living room, I sat down on the brown leather couch and began sifting through the pamphlets that the midwife had given me. One in particular stood out. Entitled *When Your Baby Dies*, it was straight to the point, brusque almost, considering that its readers would have just lost a son- or daughter-to-be. The title came across as particularly heartless. In fact, seeing it made me feel physically sick. My stomach squirmed. I sprang up from the couch, ran to the kitchen, and proceeded to throw up large amounts of bile into the sink. After a few more violent bursts of puking up the yellowish, bitter-tasting fluid, the nausea passed. I turned the cold tap on full, splashed some freezing water over my face and drank some straight from the nozzle. The chill made my sensitive teeth twinge and my sore stomach go into spasm.

I rested on the couch for a while. When I felt strong enough, I picked up the telephone and our address book. The book was small, only just bigger than my hand, with a burgundy-red leather cover that felt smooth and cold. It was a housewarming gift from Sarah's parents, and now I was going to use it to break the terrible news to them.

Should I call them first or maybe my own parents? Who would be easier to tell? Who would take the news bravely? In the end, I decided to call Sarah's parents first, thinking that it would be slightly easier as they weren't my flesh and blood. I was wrong. It proved to be extremely difficult. My fingers slipped as I began punching in the numbers. I misdialled twice in a row before composing myself and doing it correctly.

The phone rang and rang. I was about to hang up when finally my call was answered. Sarah's mother greeted me. I got straight to the point. My vocal cords were all over the place as I broke the news to her. She didn't take it well. She cried hysterically, and when I spoke to Sarah's father, I could still hear her crying in the background, her dreams of a grandson banished in the ten seconds it had taken me to tell her. Sarah's father, on the other hand, was more reserved. I could tell that he was mightily upset, but he was the old-fashioned sort, strong and reserved, and he took the bad news square on the chin. He asked whether we wanted them to come over and comfort us, but I politely declined his offer. Sarah was better left alone to catch up on some much-needed rest. The day had brutalised her. I asked him if they could tell her sister what had happened; then I said my goodbyes and hung up.

I felt too drained to go through it all again, but I had to. Without breaking stride I dialled my parents' number straight away. My mother answered, her voice full of joy when she recognised mine. Like Sarah's mother, she was looking forward to being a grandmother for the first time, and must have thought that this was the call to give her the good news. After I'd devastated her with the opposite, she fell silent. I asked whether she was still there, and when she eventually replied she asked me, of all things, if I was joking. How she could possibly think I would joke about something like that was beyond me, but I informed her that it was the truth, and then that we were going back to the hospital in a few days' time for Sarah to give birth to our stillborn baby, her stillborn grandson.

After talking for a while longer, exchanging condolences, I asked whether my father was there. He wasn't. He was out buying some wood from a DIY store to build a new fence or something like that. I told her that I had to go, and asked her to pass on the news to him. Before I hung up, she told me how sorry she was for both of us and said we should keep our chins up. She told me that time is a healer. That was the end of the conversation.

To try to pass some time, I turned on the television. Each programme that I came across was a comedy, full of laughter and smiling faces. But nothing would lift my mood that night. It would be utterly impossible. I flicked through the channels for hours on end, without really watching anything in particular, keeping my eyes fixed on the moving pictures until they grew weary and I had exhausted myself. There was no way I'd be able to sleep that night otherwise.

It was a couple of seconds after midnight when I went through to our room. Sarah was lying on top of the bed where I'd left her. She was fully dressed and still curled up into a ball. I didn't bother getting undressed either. I lay down next to her and wrapped my arms around her belly. Although I desperately wanted to sleep, I couldn't drift away. There was too much going on in my mind, too many thoughts and emotions flying around my brain. Lying there with my eyes open, I stared at the cot that I had assembled for James only a few weeks earlier. It stood next to the bed, on Sarah's side. I imagined what it would have been like if he had lived. I thought about what our future would have been, how our lives would have changed. I thought about James having a little brother or sister somewhere down the line. I thought about his first steps, his first words, his first birthday, his first girlfriend, his first heartbreak, his wedding, and his own children. I thought about a lot of things, way too many things, and in between those thoughts, I drifted in and out of sleep.

# three devastating days

The three days that we had to wait until the delivery were the longest I'd ever experienced. Each day we struggled to comprehend what had happened to us. We needed to remind ourselves regularly that Sarah's large pregnant belly now harboured only the lifeless shell of our son. That horrible thought was played on repeat in my head. In a loop it went round and round, over and over, and I couldn't shift it. Each night it was a struggle to sleep, but somehow we did, and somehow we made it through the days.

On the third morning when I woke, I stretched myself awake and let out an almighty yawn. My mouth gaped so wide that it hurt my jaw. When I opened my heavy eyes, I was blinded by a burst of winter sunshine that beamed through the bedroom window and lit up our dim inhospitable room. I got out from under the warm sheets. In my underwear, I stood and gazed out of the window. The sun was shining, though there was no warmth coming from it. The ground outside sparkled with frost. I looked around to see what was going on in the neighbourhood, but it was quiet. The only active bodies I could see were two young females of roughly Sarah's age.

They were walking together, each pushing a pram in front of them. The fucking irony! They were chatting busily and would occasionally stop walking to let out explosions of laughter. They looked on top of the world. I promptly closed the curtains, glad that I, rather than Sarah, had witnessed them. I didn't think she would have been able to handle it. In my mind, I had an image of her running outside and beating the shit out of them, scratching their faces with her fingernails, tearing their hair out and spitting on them. It was unrealistic, but disturbing nonetheless, and I promptly blocked out any other such images that tried to surface. That would have, and should have, been her in a few weeks' time. She should have been one of those females, but for whatever reason it wasn't meant to be.

I walked through to the kitchen and put the kettle on. I made myself a black coffee with two sugars, and for Sarah a cup of weak tea. I took it through to her. She was still in a deep sleep, so I sat on the edge of the mattress and gently nudged her awake. She opened her eyes and smiled at me. The expression of happiness on her face took me utterly by surprise, but it was all too brief. I could see her remembering what had happened. The corners of her mouth turned down. She sank back against the pillows, all her energy gone. I kissed her on the cheek and placed her cup of tea on the bedside unit.

'How are you feeling this morning? Any better?' I enquired.

'I had a dream. A good one. And then I woke up and remembered it all. He's still dead, isn't he?' she asked, already knowing the answer but hoping to hear something else.

'Yes, he is. I'm so sorry,' I said, and kissed her again. She started to cry.

'I don't want to go to the hospital, not today. I'm too scared. I don't want to let him go. Can't I just keep him for another day or so? I don't want to lose him.'

'I'm sorry, but we need to go. The hospital has it all organised. Plus, the sooner you get this over and done with, the better you'll feel, I promise. You have to try and be brave.'

'I don't think I can get through this, I really don't.'

'Of course you can, and I'll be with you every step of the way. I'll be by your side right from the start to the very end. I won't leave you, not for a second.'

'I'm so scared … I've never felt so scared in all my life. I'm absolutely terrified.'

'I know you are. I'm scared too, but you need to do this.'

'Okay,' said Sarah. She put out her hand to me. I took hold of it and kissed it.

'You can do this, I know you can.' I followed my words up with a tender hug.

She spent a little longer in bed, tossing and turning. Once she was up and about, she showered and changed into some maternity jogging bottoms along with a baggy T-shirt. She wanted to be as comfortable as possible to help her face the strenuous day ahead. While she was sorting herself out, I packed a bag for her containing the things she might need – clothes, slippers, toiletries.

The hospital appointment was for ten o'clock. My nerves were at full throttle by then. I was a wreck. God only knows how Sarah felt. We were met by the same midwife who had broken the news of James's death to us. Once we were settled, she outlined what needed to happen.

It was nearly time to start. We were taken to a private room, one that was hidden away from the other expectant mothers. They helped Sarah on to a bed and made sure she was comfortable. Various staff members were there and tried their best to calm her with words of encouragement.

They induced her. Things started happening soon after, but in the end the labour lasted hours. I couldn't give you specifics about how long it all took, but it was definitely hours. Sarah was hurting, we all were, but it was worse for her by far. She was covered in sweat, her face creased and desperate-looking. She had the aid of an epidural, but from where I was, it didn't look to be working. She tried her best to hide the pain from me, but it was impossible to disguise. True to my word, I didn't leave her side. Most of the time I held her hand. I could feel her fear transmitting itself to me. It was a strange, surreal situation. All that effort, all that pain, all of what she was going through would eventually be for nothing. For a child who was already dead. It wasn't right. It was crushing.

Eventually James was born. As expected, he was still. I looked at his small lifeless body and began crying harder than I ever had in my life. My tear-filled eyes focused on his tiny fingers and tiny toes. I was looking for some movement, just one minuscule movement, but my heart was waiting on a miracle that I knew in my head would never come. His blue-veined eyelids remained firmly shut. There was no life for him at all, but he looked peaceful. That was something to hold on to at the very least. My beautiful young wife lay in the hospital bed, exhausted, heartbroken. Tears were streaming down her face, which was red from effort and blotched with burst blood vessels.

She held him first. She kissed his forehead and told him that she'd always love him, that he'd always be in her heart for as long as she lived. I held him and reiterated pretty much word for word the same things. Although we'd never get to see his first steps or hear his first words, he would always be a part of our lives, and I, like Sarah, would love him forever. We spent as long as we could with our baby James, trying desperately to take in every little thing about him, every tiny detail, every single attribute that he had. Our proof that he had existed in the world.

We were told that he weighed nine pounds, three ounces, and that was much bigger than anyone had anticipated, given the size of Sarah and me. The sparse hair on his head was black like mine, and I swear I could see my own features in his infant face. Or maybe that was what I wanted to see. They gave us as much time as we needed with him. They even asked whether we wanted some photographs taken with him, but we didn't feel like that would be the right thing to do. Would they have expected us to smile for the camera? Months or years down the line, I didn't want to look back at a picture of my dead baby son. The memories would be bad enough. This certainly wasn't a day I wanted to commemorate.

Eventually we had to accept our loss and hand him back. It didn't sink in straight away that we would never see him again. That today would be it, our only experience of our son.

We spent that night in hospital. Sarah was too shattered to leave, physically, psychologically, and emotionally. She told me to go home and get a proper night's sleep, but I couldn't leave her, not after all she'd been through. For the entire night I sat on the plastic-covered chair next to her bed, a blanket draped across me, drifting in and out of sleep. I was surprised I managed any at all. I was surprised either of us did. Maybe it was down to sheer exhaustion, but I was definitely grateful for the respite.

* * *

The next morning I was woken once again by the November sunshine. It flooded the white walls and reflected on my face. It felt warm against my skin. I sat staring out of the window for a while, vacantly gazing at the oncoming sunbeams and the sky that they were shining down from. Sarah woke up not long afterwards, her eyes dazed-looking and deeply shadowed. Her face was pale; she looked ill. I felt so sorry for her.

We got our things together, about to leave. On the way out we were abruptly stopped by the midwife, who explained that we still had things to do. Apparently we must register the birth and the death of our son, James. I had to ask her to run this by me a second time. I was struggling to understand what she was telling us. I didn't want it to be the truth.

Sarah broke down, screaming and shouting at the midwife. She had been through enough already. I tried calming her and sat her down in the same chair as I had slept in, telling her to take deep breaths and count to ten. Then I went out into the corridor with the midwife, who explained things to me again in all their depressing detail. She advised that it was a legal requirement, that if after twenty-four weeks of a pregnancy a baby is stillborn, it needs to be registered. In her most convincing tone she tried telling me that it was a good thing, acknowledging the fact that our little James had been alive, that he had truly existed in our lives, and that we were his parents, and that's how it would go down in the history books. It would be forever. Her strong, confident voice failed to convince me though.

After this, she put out her hand, offering me the Medical Certificate of Stillbirth along with some other damned paperwork. I didn't want to take any of it but I didn't have a choice in the matter. I snatched it all from her. She ignored my attitude, or accepted it, and carried on talking. She spoke about getting a post mortem done to see whether they could determine the cause of death. But what good would that be to anyone? I declined the offer, knowing that Sarah would feel the same.

I turned my back on the midwife and went to fetch my wife. I grabbed Sarah by the hand and practically pulled her out of the chair. With my other hand, I picked up her bag. We were stopped at the doorway by the midwife, who had produced a wheelchair. She offered to wheel Sarah to the car, but my wife declined this hands down. She didn't want to feel incapable.

Although the midwife had been the bearer of the most tragic and horrible news, she had been supportive to us throughout the whole ordeal. I apologised to her for my anger, and thanked her for the care she had taken of Sarah. Then we left.

On our way out of the maternity ward, we passed endless couples with smiling faces, the women soon-to-be loving mothers and the men proud fathers. Instead of leaving the hospital that day with a son, we left with pieces of paper and a pair of broken hearts.

We got home just after lunchtime and hardly said a word to each other for the rest of the day. What could we say? I wondered whether our lives would ever be normal again, whether we would be able to get back to how we were before, but I wasn't confident of it. When Sarah got back to the flat, she got straight into bed. I went to the kitchen and looked in the fridge. I took out a bottle of lager and started drinking. I pretty much downed that one in a single gulp and took out another. I ended up drinking every bottle in the fridge, about a dozen or so. Sitting in the living room, in silence, in darkness, I drank the night away. Between beers I sobbed. I talked to myself. I asked questions and tried to answer them hopefully. I was struggling to take in the whole gut-wrenching situation. I fought with my overactive mind, trying to find some sort of closure with all that had happened, but I couldn't. I felt lost. That night, Sarah didn't move from the bed and we didn't speak to each other. At some point I stumbled through to the bedroom, crawled under the covers, and passed out. That day and that night, I felt so bad, so worthless.

# dismantle

The following morning I had a horrendous hangover. There was a sharp pain in my right temple. It felt as if my brain was scratching against the inside of my skull. My eyes weren't working either. It was hard to focus them on anything. I turned on to my side and through the hangover haze saw Sarah lying next to me, still asleep. To my surprise, the expression on her face was about the happiest I'd ever seen. Maybe her dreams would provide an escape for her, so I decided to leave her undisturbed for as long as possible.

Seeing her face lit up that way made me feel a little happier, but then I looked beyond her and saw the cot, the empty cot. It reminded me of James and what we wouldn't have. The fresh white blankets that were in it would never be slept in, and the teddy bears that were there would never be cuddled or cherished. We had no need of the cot anymore, none at all, so I decided to dismantle it. The longer it stayed there, the longer it would hurt us. Each and every day it would serve as a harsh reminder of what we had lost, and I couldn't handle that.

Later that morning, Sarah got out of bed and joined me in the living room. She'd been asleep for a long time but still seemed tired. Her eyelids looked weighed down, and the expression I'd seen on her face earlier was gone. It was completely untraceable.

'Are you feeling okay?' I asked.

'I don't know. I don't know what to feel.'

'I know what you mean.'

'I feel empty, I guess,' she said, unconsciously wrapping her arms around her empty belly as she spoke. 'I can't stop thinking about him. I don't know what to do now.'

'Me neither.'

'It doesn't feel real. None of this does. It doesn't feel like yesterday actually happened. It's all one horrible big blur.'

'I know. It's going to take a while for us to get over it. We just need to be strong and stick together as much as possible,' I told her. But she didn't reply, so I spoke again. 'Do you mind if I do something today? I wanted to ask you before I went ahead with it.'

'What do you want to do?'

'I was going to dismantle the cot. I really want to get rid of that thing.'

'Why do you want to do that?'

'We don't need it anymore, do we? And every time I look at it I'm reminded … hurt. It's like it's taunting us, don't you think?'

'Yeah, I suppose you're right.'

'So you don't mind then?'

'No, if that's what you want to do, then go ahead.'

'I'm going to do it now then – are you sure you don't mind?'

'I don't care. You do what you like.'

'Are you sure?'

'Christ, Mark! How many times do I have to say it? You can do what you like.'

'Right then – I'd better look out my tools. I've not used them in years.'

Leaving Sarah in the living room, I went into a small box room that we used mainly for storage. It was where we kept the vacuum cleaner and other cleaning crap, along with old junk or things of sentimental value that we didn't yet feel like throwing away. I rummaged through the piles of miscellaneous items until I found my toolbox. It was an old steel one, handed down to me by my father after he'd upgraded his to a more modern style with additional compartments. Despite its petite size, mine was deceptively weighty. It was too heavy for me to haul far. As I wasn't very good at building or fixing things, I hadn't had much use for a toolbox. Until now.

I struggled through to the bedroom with it and dumped it on the bed, where it bounced on the springy mattress. I sat down next to it and looked at the cot.

That fucking thing had been nothing but trouble right from the start. We'd bought it from IKEA, and I remember spending hours in that gigantic shithole of a place, noisy and frenetic. We got lost numerous times before we found the right part of the store. There were so many hyperactive kids running about, screaming and crying, knocking things over and getting in the way of all the frustrated adults, that it made me question our sanity in deciding to have a baby of our own. The place made me feel claustrophobic and angry. As a result, I had an argument with Sarah about which cot to buy. Really, I didn't care what it looked like, but because I was so irritated by the whole experience I took my annoyance out on her, which I know wasn't fair or the right thing to do. But at the time, I couldn't help myself. I lost my rag. In the middle of the store, we argued loudly in front of an inquisitive audience, all for no real reason. Once things calmed down to a dull simmer of anger, we made a decision on which one to buy, quickly paid for it and left the store. As we left, I made a promise to myself never to set foot in that dungeon again.

When we arrived home, we were both firmly stuck in our ugly moods, regularly exchanging scouring looks with one another. I left it a few days before attempting to assemble the cot. By then, Sarah and I were back to normal: we were our happy selves again. The cot came with some very detailed instructions, written in gibberish. Or at least they were meaningless to me. I put them to one side and investigated the additional materials that came along with the main frame. I was stumped, totally clueless. I had no idea how I would manage to put it together, but I gave it my best shot.

It took nearly an entire day for me to complete it. By the time it was assembled there was a whole bunch of leftover screws and bolts that I didn't know what to do with, but it seemed stable and safe enough. The construction process had involved a lot of trial and error, and even more swearing and shouting. Sarah didn't help much; she enjoyed watching me struggle. She sat on the bed, relaxed, stress-free, with a cup of tea in her hand, reading a magazine – when she wasn't having a good laugh at the expression on my face. I didn't find it amusing. When I finally set the thing up, I was overjoyed and proud of myself. All we needed now was for the baby to arrive, and then our family would be complete. It would be perfect, I thought.

Instead, the time had arrived for me to take the thing apart and say goodbye. I took a star screwdriver from the toolbox and started undoing one of the small screws. After all the alcohol I'd drunk the night before, I had the shakes. I couldn't steady my hand, and as I turned the screwdriver, it kept on jumping out of the screw head. It took me a fair few minutes to get that one screw undone, and I knew I didn't have the patience to do that for the whole cot. There must have been about twenty or thirty of them in total, which would have taken a novice like me a good couple of hours, so I decided on a different method. A quicker and more effective one.

I went back to the toolbox and took out a hammer. I stood beside the cot, took one last look at it, and then began raining down hammer blows. Each one that connected made me feel slightly better. I totally lost myself, screaming and roaring, calling the cot all sorts of names and swearing at it. I was like a man possessed.

It took me less than five minutes to destroy the entire thing. I stood over the splintered wood and bent screws, and I felt nothing but relief.

Behind me, I heard the sound of a creaking floorboard. When I turned around, Sarah was standing in the doorway, watching me. She didn't say anything but shook her head and walked away. It was obvious that she was disappointed by my psychotic behaviour. I gathered all the pieces of broken wood together, put them in a black bin bag, and took it downstairs to the wheelie bin. That was the end of the fucking cot, and good riddance to it.

# my son is nothing but paperwork

The days that followed were worse. Our loss was beginning to sink in, reality biting hard. Sarah and I were both struggling to cope. We found it hard even to look at or talk to one another. We didn't know what to say. What could we say? When we bumped into each other throughout the flat we acted like strangers. Out of politeness, we exchanged nods and glances, like we would with a neighbour. But that was as far as it went.

To make matters worse, we also had the ordeal of visiting the register office, where we had to record the stillbirth. It was a grim prospect, the bleakest of bleak. I made the call to book an appointment. A woman answered, and in a monotonous, overly professional voice reeled off a list of paperwork we were required to take along with us. We needed to take the Medical Certificate of Stillbirth. Along with that, she required the place, date, and time of delivery, the baby's full name and our full names as well as our occupations, address, dates of birth and, finally, our marriage details and marriage certificate. Why they needed to know all this was beyond me. It was unbelievable, an absolute joke. What did my occupation have to do with my son being stillborn?

Although neither of us wanted to go, we had no choice in the matter. It had to be done. Sarah didn't get changed.

She wore the same old maternity jogging bottoms and the same old tatty T-shirt. She didn't have a shower and didn't put any make-up on. I wanted to say something, but it didn't seem worth causing her further upset. If that was how she wanted to go, then so be it.

The register office was in Leith. I drove us there. Due to the roadworks that constantly clogged up the city, it took forever to get there. When we did arrive, we checked in at reception and sat patiently in the waiting area.

It was a dire place. The carpet was old and brown, the walls a discoloured shade of yellow, well overdue for refurbishment. The neglected surroundings didn't help our mood. There were a number of other people waiting, and they all looked as glum as we did.

We didn't have to sit there long before an elderly gentleman retrieved us from the waiting area. He shouted our surname then led us in silence down a short hallway and into his office. Still without talking, he pulled out a couple of chairs for us and then sat down behind his desk.

His head was bald but for the few remaining thin white strands smoothed across it in a vain attempt to conceal his hair loss, one that wasn't worth his poor efforts; plus, he looked too old to be worrying about his appearance in any case. His face and forehead were wrinkled, his skin red and flaking. He looked like a man of the world; he certainly smelled like one, like wet grass or moss. He was a man with grit, but a man whose best years were well and truly behind him.

He didn't seem to feel sorry for us. For him, this was clearly just a job: something he dealt with on a regular basis. But our lives and our future had just been ripped apart. I think I was expecting some show of sympathy from him. Its absence was an unwelcome surprise. He took us through the process, the paperwork, and when he wasn't talking to us he would mumble to himself under his breath. For most of the time we stayed silent, only speaking when spoken to. Once he'd done everything that needed to be done, he gave us the Certificate for Burial. He handed it to me. I wanted to refuse it, like I had the Medical Certificate of Stillbirth. This was now the second certificate we had been given to affirm our son's death. They should really rename them. To me, a certificate is like an award, something to be handed out when someone has achieved something, recognition of work well done – none of which applies when you want to bury someone.

The appointment didn't even last an hour, and I felt strangely guilty about that. It felt like the less time we spent in there, the less important James was. We left with our certificate in hand and began the stop-start journey home, back through all the roadworks.

By this point in the day, my stomach was beginning to ache with hunger. Without consulting Sarah, I took a small detour to the McDonald's drive-thru close to our flat. As I drove under the golden arches, I asked her whether she wanted anything but she declined. She said she wasn't hungry, but surely she must have been. Since the birth, the death, she hadn't eaten anything proper at all, just dry toast and cereal, and sometimes the odd bowl of minestrone soup if her stomach was feeling up to it. Her lack of appetite was something I was beginning to worry about. She was looking thinner and unhealthier with each passing day. At the window, I gave my order to a typical McDonald's worker: teenaged, spotty, rude and crude. In case Sarah changed her mind and decided to eat something, I ordered a few extra sides. Back at the flat, I vegetated on the couch, watching TV and stuffing my face with comfort food. Sarah retired to the bedroom and stayed there. She didn't eat anything.

Once I'd eaten, I felt bloated and had the junk-food sweats, but it had tasted good and was definitely worth the after-effects. I decided, belatedly, to check in with the Royal High School where I taught. I picked up the phone. After two rings a familiar voice answered: it was Joan, the receptionist. She recognised my voice immediately and asked how everything was, but I didn't answer. Then she told me how worried they had been not to have heard a single word from me. But again I refused to give away any information. Instead, I asked sharply to be put through to the rector, George, and she transferred my call without saying anything more. I think she could tell by my voice that something bad had happened.

'Hello, Mark. How are you? We've not heard from you in a while,' said George.

'I know. I'm sorry that I haven't called before this but Sarah and I had some bad news … some terrible news actually.'

'What – what is it?'

'Our baby, it was stillborn.'

The line fell silent.

Eventually he replied, 'Jesus Christ! I'm so sorry to hear that, Mark. That's awful news.'

'That's why I had to leave without warning. Sarah called to tell me that she was on her way to the hospital, so I just left.'

'I understand.'

'I know I shouldn't have left my class unattended, but there was only one thing on my mind.'

'That's absolutely fine, Mark. There's no need to worry about it.'

'I really should have called earlier, though.'

'That's okay.'

'And I'm sorry I didn't reply to your texts or voicemails, but things have just been crazy since it all happened.'

'There's no need to apologise, honestly. I would have been the same.'

'Thanks, George. Thanks for being so understanding.'

'How's Sarah holding up?' he asked.

'Not good. She's a wreck actually.'

'Well, how about you take some time off to be with her … support her?'

'But I've already been at home for a good while.'

'Yeah, but what the hell. You need to be with your wife. You can take as much time off as you need.'

'Are you sure that's okay, George?'

'I most certainly am.'

'Thank you so much. I really appreciate it.'

'No problem whatsoever.'

'George, do you think you could do me one more favour?'

'Of course – fire away.'

'Could you tell the rest of the faculty what has happened? I don't think I'll be able to speak to them each individually when I do come back. It would be too much for me.'

'Absolutely. I can do that for you. No problem.'

'I can't thank you enough, George. I really can't.'

We spoke for a while longer about other things, mostly what had been happening in the school, but my focus was steadily waning. Luckily, I heard the school bell ringing in the background and the rector told me that he had to go. We exchanged our goodbyes and hung up.

I went back to watching the TV, and for the next few days that was all I would do. I would eat, drink, cry, watch TV, cry again, and then go to sleep. Sarah would occasionally appear from her slumbers and join me, but she'd sit on a chair on the other side of the room instead of snuggling up to me on the couch, like she always used to do before. I could feel her drifting further and further away from me. Somehow, I needed to start pulling her back.

* * *

We started receiving bundles of sympathy cards through the post. The first few that arrived I handed to Sarah. I wanted her to open them so she would realise that people were there for her. But she didn't want any cards. They remained unopened. It was a son she wanted, a son she couldn't have. No amount of sympathy was going to change that so the cards meant nothing to her. They were only words on thick paper. In the end, I opened all the messages of condolence.

Unwanted visits from our families were becoming all too frequent even though all we wanted was to be left alone. Sarah's mother and father were the first to come. Her father, Peter, told us that he would take care of the funeral, all the organising and expenses. He told us that we shouldn't have to burden ourselves with such a horrible chore, and I was more than happy to let him take the lead. I was grateful for it, in fact. As we all sat in the living room, Peter met my eyes then glanced deliberately towards the open door. He rose from the couch, tall and steady on his size-twelve feet, and made an announcement in his deep voice.

'Mark and I are going to have a chat, man to man. We'll be in the kitchen if you need us.'

He stomped through and I followed, closing the living-room door behind me. In the kitchen, we both sat down at the table.

'How's Sarah doing?' he asked, adding, 'She looks a wreck.'

'Badly,' I admitted. 'She's not spoken to me much and she's not been eating properly.'

'I see,' he said, stroking his chin.

'For most of the day and all of the night, she just stews in bed. I'm pretty worried about her.'

'I didn't think she'd be able to cope with it. We all need to look after her, but you especially. You need to be there for her.'

'Of course. I'm her husband,' I replied, slightly annoyed to be told how to treat my own wife.

'I'm just saying ... she's never been that strong. Emotionally, I mean. I remember when my mother – Sarah's grandmother – died, she couldn't deal with it at all. She didn't understand. She was quite young at the time, maybe eleven or twelve, and had to stay off school for two weeks. We tried forcing her to go, but ultimately we couldn't. Like you said, she would just stay in her room and mope. She'd spend hour upon hour looking through old photographs and I think that made her feel worse. She's going to find this really hard too.'

'I can't force her to do anything she doesn't want to do, though.'

'I know you can't. All I'm saying is that you'll need to look out for her ... really look after her.'

'I will.'

He fretted over Sarah for a little longer, and then we talked about the plans for the funeral. It was a dismal conversation. Once we'd said all that we had to, we went back to the living room. Sarah and her mother were sitting close together. Her mother, Sandra, had her arms wrapped around her and they were both crying. I looked at Peter, and we both walked over to our respective wives and consoled them. Soon after that, the crying stopped and Sarah's parents left the flat. After waving them off from the living-room window, Sarah returned to the bedroom and lay in the dark on our unmade bed. It felt like I was losing her a little bit more, day by day.

# a tiny funeral

It was Saturday. The day we had hoped would never arrive. When I woke, I reached across to Sarah's side of the bed, but she wasn't there. For the first time in a long while, she was awake before me. There was a strange feeling in the air. I sensed it immediately. I listened intently for any sounds, but couldn't hear a thing. Then, out of nowhere, came a retching noise. I leaped out of bed. In the bathroom I found Sarah, on her hands and knees, bent over the toilet, throwing up into the bowl. I asked her how she was, but she couldn't answer due to her vomit-filled mouth, and she continued being sick. Crouching down beside her, I rubbed her back in a circular motion. When she couldn't vomit anymore, she lay down on the tiled floor, exhausted. Sick covered her chin and there was a crusted coating around her lips. I took a towel from the rail, dampened it, and then raised her head and wiped her mouth clean. After that I picked her up and carried her through to the bedroom. She flopped back on the bed, seemingly powerless to move. She fell back to sleep for a while. When it was time for us to get ready, I woke her.

I picked out some clothes for her, ones that were suitable for the forthcoming occasion. As we dressed we didn't speak. I noticed that Sarah's arms and legs were shaking as she tried to put on her clothes and then her shoes. Once she was fully dressed, I went across and hugged her.

'Don't worry,' I said. 'I'm here for you.'

She began crying and then held on to me as tightly as she could. Her grip around me was so suffocating that I had to gasp for air.

* * *

The funeral itself was short and unpleasant. There was a tiny coffin. I imagined James's frail body lying in it, decomposing, and it frightened me. It didn't seem natural, putting this white wooden box into the soil, six feet under. We handed in some personal belongings, so they could be put in the coffin beside him. Neither of us felt strong enough to see our boy again – it had been bad enough at the hospital – so the undertaker sorted it all out for us. Amongst other things, we put in some photographs of Sarah and me. Some were taken on our wedding day, but most were from the pregnancy: a time when everything was good, when we were happy and still had so much to look forward to. When James was still alive and growing. I wanted to leave him with happy memories of us.

The funeral was for family only. Some of them felt the need to hand in further items. More photos, letters, poems, and some small soft toys were put in the already crowded box along with his corpse. Everyone was tearful during the ceremony, faintly incredulous at what they were witnessing. The women were crying uncontrollably while the men fought back tears as best they could. We were trying to stay strong, trying to lead by example. I was overjoyed once it was all over. After exchanging hugs, kisses and tears in the car park, all of the different family members got into their cars and followed us back to the flat.

It was different from any other funeral. Usually at a wake you find yourself celebrating a person's life. There'll be smiles and laughter as mourners reminisce about old times and exchange funny stories about the deceased's life. But what could be said about this one? There was no life. We didn't know our son. No one did. Mostly we sat in silence, scared to speak his name. The older family members tried their best to initiate conversations about trivial things. They spoke about the weather, stories that were in the news, or about what their neighbours had been getting up to. I sat and listened, but their bullshit became increasingly annoying so I politely excused myself. Escaping to the kitchen, I poured myself a ridiculously large glass of Glenfiddich and knocked it back in one. I took a deep breath, inhaling the rich fumes, the strong, beautiful taste of alcohol, and then I poured myself another. William joined me in the kitchen. He was the fiancé of Sarah's younger sister, Penny.

'Can I get one of those?' he asked, pointing to my glass full of whisky.

'Sure. Do you want me to make it a large one?'

'Yeah, go on then. You may as well,' he replied as he loosened his black tie.

'I can't sit through there any longer. I can't sit and listen to them talk as if nothing's happened. It's bullshit, total pish,' I said as I handed him his drink.

'I know what you mean. It's been one hell of a tough day, hasn't it?'

'You can say that again. You shouldn't have to bury your own child, especially one who never got the chance to live.'

'I really don't know what to say to either of you. I feel so sorry for you both.'

'Forget it. We keep hearing that from everyone and I don't know how to reply to it anymore.'

'You don't need to,' said William, and we both downed our drinks.

'You want another one?' I asked.

'Yeah, please. Don't make it as big as the last one, though, or I'll be well on my way to being pissed.'

'Sure thing, you lightweight.'

However, I chose to ignore his request, poured him an equally large one, and placed it in his hand.

'Oh, well then, bottoms up,' he said.

'Cheers,' I replied.

We touched our glasses together and drank to better days. There was silence for a few seconds. I didn't have anything else to say, but thankfully William spoke again.

'Do you know what you're going to do now?' he asked.

'I have no idea. I guess I'll need to go back to work soon. I don't know what Sarah's going to do though.'

'She quit her job, right?'

'Yeah, she was only really working part-time, but she resigned when she got so far along with the pregnancy.'

'Is there any chance she could get her job back?'

'Maybe, but I don't think she'd want to return to that place.'

'It was an accountant's office, wasn't it?'

'Yeah. In any case, I don't think she'll be doing anything anytime soon.'

'I guess not. I've not really spoken to her today, but she seems really broken up.'

'She's barely spoken to me since it happened. I don't know what to say to her, or what else I can do to try and help her through this.'

'I wish I could give you some advice, but I don't have a clue.'

'That's okay. I'll figure something out.'

'Do you think you'll try again?' William asked.

'Try what?'

'For another baby?'

'What? It's too soon to be talking about that, way too soon.'

'Of course it is. Shit, I'm sorry! What the fuck was I thinking? What a retard.'

'Don't worry about it, man. I've said enough stupid things myself over the past few days to last a lifetime.'

'Well, if you ever want to get a pint and talk about things, just give me a shout. I'll be more than happy to join you.'

'Yeah, I think that's a good idea. Cheers.'

We drank a few more whiskies, followed by numerous cans of Tennent's Lager. We were the only ones in the flat drinking, and well on our way to being full-on drunk. Back in the living room, we got funny looks from the rest of the family, looks of concern and disappointment. The whole thing began to wind down. Gradually people filtered out of the flat, and before we knew it, it was just the two of us again, Sarah and me. She went to the bedroom, and a few minutes later I followed. She changed out of her funeral attire. In her underwear, she got into bed, wrapping the covers tightly around herself.

'How are you doing?' I asked. Another stupid question, but I couldn't help myself; I didn't know what else to say to her.

'I just want to be left alone,' was her answer.

'Are you sure?'

'Yes, I'm certain.'

'Right, I'll speak to you in the morning.'

'Okay.'

'That's it all over now. Things will get better.'

'You think?' she said, sarcastically.

'Yeah, I'm sure of it.'

'Well, I'm not.'

She rolled over, lying on her chest, face down on the pillow. All I could see was the back of her head.

'Goodnight,' I said.

I left her alone and returned to the kitchen to retrieve the bottle of whisky. It was about half full. I went to the living room, sat on the couch, and drank in silence, straight from the bottle. I didn't bother putting the TV on. I didn't even turn the lights on. Night fell, light fading fast. Eventually I found myself sitting in pitch blackness, taking uncoordinated swigs from the bottle, like a tramp on a park bench. At some point I must have passed out. When I woke, I managed to turn on a small lamp that was stationed on the table next to the couch. I looked at my watch and it was bang on midnight, not one second over. Unsteadily, swaying from side to side, I walked out of the living room and into the bedroom. I wasn't sure whether I would actually make it to the bed, but I did. And within seconds of my head hitting the pillow, I was asleep.

# he comes to me in dreams #1

I was standing there all alone in a complete void. The only thing surrounding me was the colour white. There was nothing in front of me, nothing for my eyes to see, only a world of whiteness. It was the purest shade of white that I had ever set eyes on. It was like fresh milk, or a virgin snowfall, or a polished bone. I didn't know where I was or what I was doing there. With nothing else to focus on, I looked down at my feet but I couldn't even see them. No arms, no legs, no torso – my whole body was invisible to me. However, I was definitely there, wherever 'there' was. I turned around slowly and cautiously, looking to see whether there was anything behind me. There wasn't. It was just more of the same. The same empty pointless space. And then it changed.

When I turned back to my original starting point, something was visible, far, far away in the distance. It was a mere speck, a dot, but nonetheless it was something. It was the only thing. So I began walking towards it. For a while I trekked on without drawing any closer; it remained the same distance from me. So I started running. I ran as fast as I could for as long as I could. Eventually the speck began to take shape. It was turning into something ... something of substance, something of stature.

When I was close enough to make out exactly what it was, I had to stop and take a deep breath. The sight was unbelievable. I thought my eyes were playing tricks on me, but they weren't.

The speck in the distance was our son. It was James. He was sitting there, very much alive. I ran faster than I had before. Although I couldn't see my own body, I noticed sweat flying off me and scattering over the surrounding purity. I could hardly breathe, but I didn't stop running. I wanted to get to James as quickly as I could. I felt my heart pounding against my chest. Every thumping heartbeat could be heard as it pumped faster and louder.

Then I was standing right in front of him. He was naked, a baby doing the things you'd expect a baby to do. He sucked on his fingers while drool dribbled down his chin. He burped. He crawled around aimlessly on the white ground, trying to learn the world. He looked happy. He didn't notice I was there. Maybe I was invisible to him, like I was to myself. I stood and watched, just savouring him. I saw his eyes blink, his fingers flex, his nose run. I was overcome with joy. He was so alive. Wherever he crawled, I followed. He had me under his spell.

After a while, he stopped crawling and sat still. He lifted his head and looked in my direction. I tried to talk to him. I could hear the words in my head, but they weren't being spoken aloud. Repeating his name over and over, I tried again and again but each time received no response. It angered me so much that I screamed his name.

I screamed it as loud as I could. It was a demonic scream, and I could actually hear it this time. Not just in my head, but for real. Some kind of barrier had been broken.

The noise grabbed James's attention. He was now definitely looking at me. He smiled and giggled. Lifting one of his baby arms, he put out his hand to me. I crouched down and reached for it. My arm was now visible to me. I looked down at myself and I was now there in my full body. I continued to reach for his hand, but when I finally got hold of it, he disappeared. I looked around but all trace of James was gone. I was alone again in the white wilderness. My son had been snatched from me once more. I screamed, fell to my knees, and began lashing out.

'WHY? WHY?' I roared. 'WHAT DID I DO TO DESERVE THIS?' I demanded. The answer was silence.

I cried. I couldn't stop crying. A puddle of tears widened around my knees. I tried wiping my eyes with the sleeve of my shirt, but it grew sodden and did nothing to stem the flow. The puddle grew so big that I started to sink into it. First my legs disappeared; then I was up to my waist in my own tears. I tried to grab hold of something, but there was nothing to save me. Flailing my arms and kicking my legs proved useless. Whatever I tried, I couldn't stop myself from sinking. The water was up to my neck. I took one final deep breath before my head went under.

Fully submerged now, I opened my eyes. The puddle had become an ocean, a deep blue ocean of my saltwater tears. It was calm, and still, and silent. There were no fish. There was no sea life at all. With my wavy watery vision, I could see that James had reappeared. He was swimming and smiling. Bubbles were escaping from his mouth. I swam towards him. Different strokes – front crawl, breast, butterfly – each one slow and tiring, and each one a failure. Before I reached him, all the breath had left my body. As I gasped for life, water filled my mouth. I swallowed and swallowed but eventually I gave up and drowned.

I woke up in bed, practically hyperventilating, my chest moving wildly up and down. I ran to the bathroom, knowing I was going to be sick. I didn't make it in time and threw up on the floor in the hallway. Sweat was pouring off me and my legs were shaking furiously. I wasn't sure what had happened. It was a dream, I knew that much, but it hadn't felt like one. It had felt real.

I reached the bathroom and put the light on. I looked at my face in the mirror, noticing the sweat beading my forehead. My eyes were swollen with tears. I was scared. Before I went back to bed, I forced myself to clean up the sick, so it was non-existent to Sarah. Back under the covers, my side of the bed was damp, probably with sweat. I moved my hand towards Sarah's side – it appeared to be dry. Despite the dampness, I tried to get back to sleep but couldn't. I was too apprehensive about what I might dream of. Instead, I lay on my back and stared at the ceiling. My whole body was still shaking, my heart still pounding. And James … James was still gone.

# the runner and the home straight

When I got out of bed properly, I still felt nervous and anxious. Sarah was already up, sitting in the living room in her bathrobe, watching the TV with the volume down low. I wanted to tell her about my dream but didn't think it was the right thing to do, so I kept it to myself. I tried to force it away, deep into the back of my mind. Maybe one day, when she was feeling better, I would tell her all about it, but not now. It could destroy her. She looked at me inquisitively. She could sense that something was amiss and got straight to the point.

'What's wrong with you?' she asked.

'Nothing. I'm fine,' I replied in a jittery voice.

'You don't seem fine to me. You're shaking. You look like shit!'

'I'm okay. I just didn't sleep that well.'

'Maybe you're coming down with something.'

'Honestly, I'm fine. I think I'm going to go out for a run.'

'What?'

'A run. I'm going to go out for a run.'

'Are you really?' she asked sarcastically.

'Yeah, I feel like I need to do something.'

'You've not been out running for months, and it'll be freezing outside.'

'I know all that, but it's about time I got started again, I guess. What are you going to do today?'

'Nothing. I don't feel up to doing much.'

'Right, well, I'm going to get changed and then I'm out of here.'

'Aren't you going to have something to eat first?'

'Nah, I'm not hungry. I'll get something when I get back.'

'Okay.'

She turned her attention away from me, focusing back on the television. I went to the box room. My toolbox was on top of a pile of stuff, reminding me of the day I'd destroyed the cot and the way I'd just flipped. I moved it to one side, rummaged through more junk, and found my running trainers. They were caked in dried-up mud and dirt. A fuzzy green mould had grown around the rubber soles. They smelled atrocious. The laces were still tied from the last time that I'd used them. I took them to the bedroom and set them down on the floor. I went into a drawer, took out a pair of shorts and a T-shirt, and got changed. Then I sat on the bed, picked up the trainers, untied the laces, and slipped them on to my clammy feet. I steadied my hands, which allowed me to tie the laces again, and then I got back to my feet. I jogged on the spot for a minute or so, testing them out, before returning to the living room, where I said goodbye to Sarah and left the flat.

Down the stairwell I ran, two steps at a time, while holding on to the banister. Outside, the shock of the winter temperature hit me. The thought of turning back entered my mind, retreating upstairs into the warmth and comfort of the flat again, or even going back to get a jacket, but I'd warm up after running for a while, I decided. More than likely, if I did go back inside I would not emerge again.

Most of the paths were paved with frost, but I still managed to run on them. When parts got too slippery and dangerous, I ran on the gritted roads instead. My destination was unclear. I didn't know where I was running to. There was no predetermined route. My only aim was to use up as much of my nervous energy as I could. First, I ran up to the main street of Corstorphine, St. John's Road, past all the shops, the pubs and the people. As I went by, I looked in the windows and could see families having lunch together, couples kissing, children laughing or crying. I ran down towards Murrayfield, passing the zoo, the rugby stadium, and the ice rink. In the fields opposite the stadium, people were walking their dogs, boys were playing football on the hardened grass, and couples were walking hand in hand, enjoying their Sunday strolls in the brisk air. I got to Haymarket and ran beyond the train station. The closer I came to the heart of the city, the more tourists I found surrounding me. It felt like they were invading my space, invading my hometown.

When I reached Princes Street, it proved difficult to avoid running into people. I tried my best, but it turned out not to be good enough. As I ran, I looked up at Edinburgh Castle, a landmark that should have filled me with pride, but felt nothing. It wasn't important to me anymore. It was just a building made from stone and sand and nothing more, a superficial monument without a soul. I kept running, and continued bumping into people. Most of them just glared at me, but the more confident, younger ones pushed me and shouted at me. They would yell things like 'arsehole' or 'faggot', but I had zoned out. I paid no attention to their jibes, and didn't retaliate. Although I didn't want to, I remembered the dream. The thoughts it conjured up were unavoidable, and the more I dwelt on them, the harder and faster I ran. I went up and over the South Bridge and continued on. The chilling air had turned my arms red, and my toes were growing numb, but that didn't stop me. I just ran.

In total, I must have been running for over two hours before I eventually halted. I had no idea where I was anymore. On the unknown pavement, on the unknown street, I hunched over, rested my hands on my knees and tried to catch my breath. My nose was running as if I had a heavy cold, and a feverish sweat dripped from me.

I turned around and looked in the direction I had just come from. The prospect of running all the way back to the flat was harrowing. I'd probably collapse or take a heart attack before I made it home. Plus, my legs were now very weak. They felt like jelly, jelly that hadn't even set. I sat down on the pavement, leaning my back against a wall. For a while I stayed there. I had no choice but to rest. As I did so, I could feel drops of rain falling from the sky, settling on my bare-skinned arms and legs. There were black clouds overhead. They looked to be full of rain, and they covered the sky for as far as my tired eyes could see. Shortly after, it began pouring down. It was torrential. I struggled to my feet and walked on, further into the unknown location that I'd found myself lost in, looking for shelter. To my relief, I found a small grocery store on the next corner. As I opened the door, a bell rang. There was an Asian man standing behind the counter, reading a newspaper. He lifted his head momentarily to give me a suspicious glance. I stood in the doorway, not moving. I didn't want to get his floor wet.

'Do you mind if I stand here for a few minutes, to see if the rain passes?' I asked.

He shrugged his shoulders and went back to reading his newspaper. I stood and hoped, but hope wasn't enough. The rain didn't stop. It didn't even ease. My back was close to the door. All of a sudden, I felt the door swing into me and I jumped out of the way. As the bell rang, an old lady entered the shop. Compared to me, she was tiny. She wore a plastic rain bonnet on her head to protect herself from the heavy downpour. She took it off, revealing a well-constructed helmet of grey hair, still perfectly arranged despite the conditions outside. She looked at me, one eyebrow raised.

'Did I just hit you with the door, son?'

'Yeah, but it's my fault. I shouldn't have been standing so close to it in the first place.'

'That's right, you shouldn't have,' she said, and burst into a fit of cackling laughter, after which she began having a nasty coughing fit. She spluttered and hawked up all sorts of crap – you could hear it coming up – but after a while she composed herself.

'Are you okay there?' I asked.

'Yeah, don't worry about me. I've been like this for years. It's all down to the fags.'

'I see.'

'What are you doing out here, dressed like that?' she asked, pointing to my attire. 'You'll catch your death, you idiot!'

'I know, but I've been out running.'

'You've been out in that?' She pointed to the icy rain outside.

'Yeah, but when I left the house it wasn't so bad. It was cold, but I thought I'd be okay.'

'And when was that?'

'I'm not sure. Maybe a couple of hours ago, but I've not got a watch on me so I couldn't really tell you for sure.'

'Where did you run from?'

'Corstorphine,' I told her.

'CORSTORPHINE!' she repeated, saying it twice as loud as I had.

'Yes,' I replied.

'Why did you come all the way up here from Corstorphine? You must have a screw loose, young man.'

'Maybe I do, but I just had to get out of the house. I've had a bit of a rough time recently.'

'Well, I don't want to pry into your personal business. I don't want to know what you get up to. I don't know what's wrong with people nowadays. Everyone's gone crazy. There aren't any normal people anymore.'

'Tell me about it.'

'And how are you going to get home exactly?'

'I don't know.'

'Don't you have any money on you?'

'Nope, I didn't bring anything with me. I didn't expect to be out for this long or to come this far, as a matter of fact.'

'I could give you some money for a bus home, if you want. There's a stop just around the corner, and, luckily for you, there's a bus that'll take you right there.'

'Thanks, but I couldn't take money from a stranger. That wouldn't feel right. I'll get a taxi and pay for it when I'm dropped off.'

'Don't be daft! A taxi would cost you a small fortune, and where the hell would you get one around here? Have you looked outside? There's nothing in this dump, not a taxi rank in sight. There are practically no cars on the roads at all.'

'Maybe you're right, but I can't take money from you.'

'Listen, you seem like a nice young man, albeit a bit of a dim one, and I would like to give you some change for a bus home.'

'I'm not sure I'd be comfortable accepting anything from you.'

'Please, just take the bloody offer and stop being so damn stubborn! Anyway, it would make me feel good about myself. A good deed would be done and I don't get the chance to do one of those very often.'

'Well, only if you're absolutely sure.'

'I'm positive, one hundred per cent!'

'Well, thank you very much. That's really kind of you.'

'You need to do one thing for me though.'

'What's that then?' I asked curiously.

'You need to earn your fare. You're going to help me with my groceries. That's why I came here in the first place,' she said, handing me a green shopping basket. 'Only if you're not too exhausted from your running, that is,' she added.

'No, it would be my pleasure to help. It'll certainly be worth the fare home.'

'Well, let's get down to business then,' she said, and started walking down one of the aisles.

I had dried off ever so slightly and didn't drip on the floor too much as I followed her around the store. She brought an old receipt out of her bag, and on the back of it was a short list of things scribbled down in pencil. To me, it was illegible. She read it out loud while I collected the things from the shelves and placed them in the basket. Every now and again I'd pick out the wrong item, and she'd put on a pair of glasses, inspect the label or the packaging of the item, and tut at me before telling me to go back and get the right thing. She was a stern old lady but I liked her, and didn't take offence at her old-school attitude. If anything, I found it amusing and somewhat refreshing.

A bulging, heavy basket later, we were at the counter and the man behind it put down his newspaper and started pricing up the items, without making eye contact or saying anything to us. Once he'd put everything through, I packed the items into the plastic carrier bags that were set out on the counter. The old lady then asked the shopkeeper for a packet of cigarettes before paying for all her things. Before going back outside, we stood at the door for a few minutes, allowing her to put her rain bonnet back over her sculpted hair. Outside, the rain was still lashing down. I asked the woman whether I could carry the shopping back to her house as an extra little gesture of my appreciation, and she accepted my offer. I got the feeling she was enjoying our encounter, however slight and awkward it was.

Her house wasn't far from the store, a two-minute walk around the corner. From the outside it looked small and quaint. When we spoke, she didn't mention a husband or any family whatsoever, so I assumed she lived alone. We walked up a couple of steps to her front door and I set the bags down. She opened the door and stepped inside. I picked up the bags and put them over the threshold beside her feet, saving the groceries from getting any wetter than they already were. She invited me in for a cup of tea, but I politely declined.

As I offered my excuse, I found myself babbling on. I told her exactly what had happened to Sarah and me, how I really had to get home now, how my wife would probably be worried sick about me. The old girl understood that wholeheartedly. Taking the hint, she started rummaging around in her purse. She took out a fistful of change and handed me a mixture of silver and copper coins – plenty of them, too many for the price of a bus fare. I thanked her, but before I left, she told me to wait and then disappeared down her hallway with an air of excitement, almost skipping in her haste. Above the sounds of cupboard doors opening and closing, and banging and clattering, I could hear her talking to herself. She left me standing on the doorstep for a decent amount of time, long enough for me to feel the cold again, my arms growing pinker by the second. Soon they'd be full-on red again.

Finally she came back sporting a wide, wrinkled smile. I had no idea what she was up to or why she was so happy. Her frail hands were clasped together around something. Slowly she opened them, revealing a Mars bar. I looked at her and I think the smile on my face outstretched hers. She handed it to me. I thanked her and kissed her on the cheek. Leaving her standing on the doorstep, I walked away with a gentle spring in my step, my faith in the world ever so slightly restored. That small gesture proved to me that there was hope left and good people still existed; they were simply hard to find.

As I made my way to the bus stop, I couldn't help but keep the smile on my face. The bus shelter was deserted. I checked the timetable and a bus was due to arrive. For a change the timetable was actually correct. The wait was short, and when the bus came I got on and handed over the correct amount of change. I held the rest of the coins tightly in my clenched fist.

There were only two passengers on the bus, and they both gave me sidelong looks. One was an old man. He was wearing a long black jacket that came down to his knees, and he had a grey trilby hat on his head. He was stylish for a man of his age. By contrast the other person was a young female, possibly in her late teens or early twenties, wearing a pink hooded jumper with its hood up and a pair of grey jogging bottoms. She looked like your stereotypical teenaged mother, albeit with no child in sight. She really was a mess. Though I say that, they must have thought I was a lunatic, dressed the way I was, drenched to the skin and clutching a Mars bar as if it were the Holy Grail. All that, along with an exaggerated cartoon-like grin. They must have thought I had mental issues, that I was a special case.

I sat on a seat near the front of the bus, away from the other two passengers. I stared out of the window, watching the rain batter against it as the grey city passed by in the background. After a while my stomach began to twinge, twitch, and then rumble furiously. I hadn't eaten anything all day, so I unwrapped the Mars bar and began powering through it. I ate it too fast, chomping it down in three large bites. Saliva and caramel covered my chin, so I wiped it clean with my damp T-shirt.

It took a while for the bus to navigate its way through the city, due to roadworks, traffic, and the occasional passenger getting on or off at various stops. Soon the bus was empty; I was the only person on it, apart from the driver. We reached Corstorphine, where I got off, leaving him all alone in his large vehicle. As I stepped out I thanked him, but he didn't mutter a single word in response. He just closed the doors behind me and drove on to the next stop.

Thanks to the kindness of the old lady and her gift of a chocolate bar, I was in a much better mood. My memories of the dream had all but disappeared, and despite the rain and the grey clouds still hanging overhead, I could feel a slight breakthrough happening, sense the light at the end of the tunnel. Maybe the future didn't look so bleak after all, and maybe there would be happiness for me somewhere along the line. I was optimistic that on this occasion the cliché would prove right: time would be a healer. It was the best I'd felt since we'd lost James. Now I was on the home straight. After my epic day, I was nearly home. It only took a couple of minutes for me to walk from the bus stop back to the flat, but even that felt too long.

Excitement overwhelmed me as I entered the stairwell. The feeling of relief was indescribable. I was home, back in the warmth again, safe from the treacherous elements outside. I tried opening the front door, but it was locked. As I didn't have any keys on me, I rang the doorbell and waited anxiously for Sarah to come. She didn't. Again I rang it, and again there was no answer. I listened attentively for footsteps, but none were forthcoming. I listened for anything. Nothing.

Bending down, I peeked through the letterbox with my left eye and saw something. Our bedroom was opposite me and the door to it stood wide open. Sarah was lying on the bed, out cold. It was hard to see everything with only half my usual vision, but I noticed that there was a wine bottle lying next to her. To me it was obvious what had happened. She'd gotten drunk, so drunk that she was now unconscious. I battered the door with my fists, following that up with continuous rings of the doorbell. She didn't budge. The thought of kicking the door down ran through my head, but that would probably be an expensive option to fix. Instead, I decided to sit in the stairwell and wait for her to wake up.

It wasn't long before my exhaustively drawn-out day caught up with me. With my back against the front door, I slept. Not for long, though. My sleep was disturbed by a crashing sound. My eyelids snapped open, eyeballs almost popping out of my skull. I was wide awake now. Opening the letterbox again, I could see

Sarah staggering about the bedroom like a zombie. On the carpet was the now shattered wine bottle. How she'd smashed it I didn't know. I didn't want to know. I shouted through the letterbox and she slowly stumbled to the door and opened it.

'What the hell have you been doing?' I asked.

No answer. And if I had been her, I wouldn't have answered either. Instead, she turned her back on me and began walking towards the kitchen. I stood and observed her halting progress. Each step she took left a bloody footprint on the wooden floor.

'Jesus Christ! Look at your feet. There's blood everywhere!' I yelled.

She walked on into the kitchen and sat down on one of the wooden chairs. I ran through, avoiding the red smears that now patterned the floor.

'You've got glass in your fucking feet!' I screeched.

Raising her head, she looked at me. Her face was expressionless. She remained silent. I placed my hands on her cheeks and made sure her eyes were looking into mine.

'What are you doing to yourself?' I asked.

Letting her go, I sat down on the other wooden chair and looked at her again. She stared vacantly in the direction of one of the cupboards. Blood dripped from the soles of her feet, settling on the lino. I took out the first-aid kit and retrieved a pair of tweezers from the bathroom.

When I returned to the kitchen, Sarah remained silent

and still. Lifting her left foot from the floor, I placed it on my knee. Stuck in the sole was a shard of glass. Her skin felt frozen. With the tweezers I pulled the glass out sharply. Sarah cringed ever so slightly, which to me seemed like a good sign. It meant that she was still with me, that she could still feel, even if she acted as though she could not. The cut wasn't too deep, not bad enough for stitches. I soaked a cotton ball with some antiseptic liquid, cleaned the wound thoroughly, and then bandaged it up tightly. There was an almost identical gash on her right foot so I repeated the procedure. Once finished, I put the dirty cotton balls in the bin, cleaned my hands in the sink, and sat back down. Out of the blue, to my amazement, Sarah spoke.

'Where were you?' she asked.

'I went out running. I told you this morning that I was going out running.'

'But for this long?'

'I know. I'm sorry.'

'You've been gone all day.'

'I know. I said I'm sorry. I didn't realise I'd be so long.'

'You're my husband. You're meant to be here for me, especially at a time like this.'

'I am here for you. I'm here now, and I just bandaged your feet up.'

'Well, you weren't here earlier when I needed you most, and you didn't even take your phone with you. How was I meant to get in touch?'

'I'm sorry,' I said again. 'What more do you want me to say?'

'Just something that has some feeling in it!'

'I don't even know what you mean by that.'

'Fuck you, Mark!'

'Fuck me! FUCK ME! I'm the only one trying to get shit sorted out around here. You've just been moping around the house feeling sorry for yourself,' I said in a raised voice.

'I'm allowed to feel sorry for myself, you fucking prick!' she shouted back at me.

I could smell the wine on her breath. She got to her feet and walked over to the kitchen sink.

'Yeah, but you can't stay like this forever – it's not going to do you any good. It's not going to do *us* any good. I certainly don't think getting drunk on a Sunday afternoon is going to sort any of our problems out, do you?'

'You're an insensitive piece of shit!' she screamed over her shoulder.

I walked towards her. She had her hands on the counter, head down, tears raining from her eyes.

'I'm really, really sorry,' I said, talking to the back of her head. 'Listen, I won't go away again. If you need me, just let me know and I'll be there for you.'

I put my hands on her shoulders but she backed into me forcefully. Her action caught me off guard. I was knocked off balance and stumbled all the way over to the other side of the small kitchen. I only stopped when my back crashed into the fridge door. She turned around.

'I shouldn't have to tell you to be there for me – you should always be there for me!'

Her right hand disappeared into the sink momentarily before reappearing, clutching a dirty bread knife.

'Sarah, what the hell are you doing with that?'

She didn't reply. The look on her face! I'd never seen her eyes like that before – red-tinged, full of fury. I didn't move. I dared not. We were at a stand-off. I hoped that she would come to her senses and realise exactly what she was doing, but it didn't work out like that. She waved the knife around rhythmically, as if she were conducting an orchestra or performing tricks in a magic show. The rhythm stopped. She launched herself at me. In a single movement, I jumped out of the way and managed to remove the knife from her hand.

I held her pinned against the chilled door until she calmed. With her face pressed up against various fridge magnets, I told her that I loved her. I told her that I was sorry. I told her that we could get through this. I told her that we needed to stick together. I told her, I told her, I told her. And after I'd said what I had to, she crumbled, turned around, and hugged me.

'I'm so sorry, Mark. I don't know what's happening to me.'

'It's okay,' I replied.

It wasn't. In all honesty, I had no idea what was happening to her either. And now I felt frightened of my own wife. Emotionally exhausted and feeling beaten up, we both retired to bed early that night.

# doctor, doctor

A couple of days went by. After Sarah's apology about the whole bread-knife fiasco, I had hoped she would start getting better, that she would see the error of her ways and her mood would change. It didn't. It went completely the opposite way. She was in a steady decline, and despite my best efforts I couldn't turn her around to start the ascent again. She didn't have the strength to pull herself out of it. As I tried to get my own life back on track, Sarah would hide away in the darkness of the bedroom, only emerging from it when it was essential: when she needed food, or a drink, or had to relieve herself. She wore the same clothes day in, day out, and would hardly wash. It wasn't healthy. The brief interludes of conversation I'd had with her previously were over now. I swear, I often went a whole day without hearing her say a single word. I thought about what I could do to help her, but knew that I couldn't manage it on my own. So I called the doctor.

My call was answered by the slow voice of an old woman. I asked her whether I could speak directly with our regular doctor as I didn't want to go through a third party or leave a message, but she informed me that Dr. Campbell was with a patient and it wasn't possible to disturb him. But she was nice enough, and, after I'd explained the situation to her, she took down my telephone number and told me that she'd get him to call me back at his earliest convenience. I gave her my mobile number. I didn't want him calling the flat in case Sarah answered. If she knew what I was up to, if she knew that I was organising a visit from the doctor, she'd go ballistic and most certainly wouldn't let it happen.

Anxiously awaiting the call, I sat in the living room with my phone clenched tightly in my hand. For some obscure reason, I was shocked when it actually rang. As the phone vibrated it fell out of my grasp, landing on the carpet. Quickly, I picked it up and answered the call while making my way out of the flat into the secret safeness of the stairwell. I spoke quietly, almost in a whisper, and explained the whole situation to him. I asked Dr. Campbell whether he could make a home visit as soon as possible as there was no way that Sarah would go to the surgery. He agreed, although it was going to be a couple of days before he'd be able to come.

* * *

He arrived on Friday, late in the afternoon. I heard his heavy footsteps echoing in the stairwell before the doorbell rang. When I opened the door to him, his breathing was laboured. He was too busy gasping for air to say much at first. He was a big man, obese actually, which in a doctor I found surprising. His flabby neck overhung the collar of his shirt, and his wobbling pot belly pushed the buttons of his shirt to bursting point.

We went through the usual formalities, greeting one another, shaking hands, and then I led him inside. We sat down in the living room. Again I explained all that had happened to us, and what was still happening to Sarah. I detailed everything – the mood swings, the loss of appetite, the sleeping, the silence. Based on that, he made a suggested diagnosis. Of course, it was depression, pure and simple. Obviously I knew she was depressed, I just didn't know how badly, and I'd always assumed that one day she'd wake up and everything would be fine, that she would somehow have snapped out of her despair and life would be back to normal again. But it didn't seem as if that day would be here anytime soon.

After discussing Sarah's mental health with the GP, I told him about the physical wounds she'd suffered. I described the punctures on the soles of her feet and how she came to get them. Finally, I had told him everything. It was time for him to see her. Feeling like a traitor, I took him to the bedroom and opened the door.

The scene we found shocked me, even though I'd slept in the room the night before. Seeing it with the doctor by my side, I felt embarrassed and ashamed. We were welcomed by a stagnant stench, one that lingered like the smell of damp. The room itself was a disgrace. For two grown adults to be living in such squalor was utterly inexcusable. Dirty clothes lay piled on the floor and the bed.

Coffee- and tea-stained cups stood on the bedside unit, while dirty plates were stacked up and scattered all over the place. Some were even balanced on the narrow windowsill. The curtains were closed and the room was in darkness. Sarah lay sleeping, undisturbed by our arrival. I woke her gently. Her eyes opened. She looked confused and shocked to find two figures standing over her.

'What's going on?' she asked. 'Who's that man?' she added, pointing to the doctor.

'It's Dr. Campbell. You remember him, don't you?'

'Yeah, I think so. But more to the point, what is he doing here?'

'He's just come to check how you're feeling. He wants to see how you're getting on.'

'I'm fine. Absolutely fine. I don't need to see a bloody doctor!'

'Come on, Sarah. You know that's not true. You're not fine at all. Just look at yourself. It's nearly dinnertime and you're still stewing in bed. You've been here for the last four days running. That's not normal, is it?'

'FUCK YOU, MARK! FUCK YOU! I DON'T NEED A FUCKING DOCTOR!' she screamed before sliding under the duvet and pulling it over her head. She was now invisible to us.

The doctor spoke. 'Sarah, I'm not here to judge you. I'm not here to cause you any grief. I just want a quick word, to see if I can help you in any way. You've been through a lot and it's quite normal for you to be feeling like this. Please, Sarah – all I want is a quick five-minute chat, and then I'll be out of your hair. What do you say to that?'

To my amazement, she gradually reappeared from under the duvet. She pulled herself back up the bed so that her head and shoulders were now in view. Reluctantly, she agreed to speak with the doctor on condition that I wasn't there to listen. I left the room. But instead of making my way to the living room, I stood in the hallway. I wanted to hear what she had to say. With my ear pressed up against the door, I listened hard, but they both spoke so softly that I couldn't make out in any detail what was being discussed. He wasn't in there long, though it was more than the five-minute chat they'd agreed on.

The conversation ended. I heard his heavy footsteps coming towards the door, and I stepped smartly through to the living room. I didn't want him knowing that I'd been eavesdropping; he wouldn't have liked that. When I heard the door creak open, I walked back into the hallway as if I hadn't just been there. We went through to the kitchen where I made him a cup of tea and offered him a selection of chocolate biscuits, of which he took the two biggest. He unwrapped one of them and as he ate it he told me that Sarah was obviously grieving over the loss of our child, and that she may also have a bout of post-natal depression tied in with it all. The diagnosis was what I had expected: it was straightforward. He had also examined the wounds on her feet, but was happy with the way the healing process was progressing and felt no further action was required. After he'd finished his coffee and his second biscuit, he filled out a prescription for a course of antidepressants. He told me to try Sarah with them first, and if things didn't improve with medication he could perhaps look at setting up some sessions with a counsellor. He'd heaved himself out of the chair and was about to leave when I jumped in with a question.

'Sorry, but before you go, can I ask you one more thing?'

'Of course. What is it?'

'Okay, here goes,' I said, and took a deep breath before continuing, 'This is going to sound stupid, possibly crazy, but … do you know much about dreams?'

'Sorry?' he said, as if he hadn't heard me correctly.

'Well, I had a strange dream a few days ago … and I mean very, very strange. It was about the baby and at the time I'd have sworn it was real. Everything about it felt so real.'

'I'm afraid that's not really my area of expertise, but you can tell me about it if you think it will help.'

'Well, the dream was about our son. His name was going to be James. I mean, his name was James.'

I was stuttering so I paused, composed myself, and carried on explaining the best I could.

'Pardon me, I'll start again. Our son's name was James. In my dream I saw him and he was far away in the distance. So I went to him, and when I got there I tried to hold his hand, but he disappeared – he just vanished into thin air. Then I began crying and sank into a puddle of my own tears, which led me to an ocean where James was swimming, but before I could swim to him, I ran out of breath and drowned. It felt so real … it felt so unbelievably real. Have you ever heard of anything like that before?'

'That's quite some dream you've had there.'

'I know. So, have you heard of people dreaming like that?'

'I've heard of some cases, not many but some. If my memory doesn't fail me, I think it's called lucid dreaming.'

'Did you say lucid dreaming?'

'Yeah, but don't quote me on that.'

'It sounds a bit sinister. What is it?'

'It's where the dreamer is fully aware that they are participating in a dream, but despite this awareness remains trapped in a dream state. Usually, though, the dreamer can participate in the dream events without limitations, without barriers. They can do as they please. That doesn't quite tie in with your experience. However, these dreams do feel extremely real and vivid, just like yours. That's about all I know, I'm afraid.'

'That's pretty interesting.'

'They're quite common when someone's been through some kind of emotional ordeal, such as the one you and Sarah have had to endure.'

'So, you don't think I should worry about it, then?'

'No, if I were you I wouldn't worry.'

'Good.'

'Also, if you've not been sleeping properly, that could be another factor.'

'Okay, thanks.'

'They'll stop in their own time.'

'I certainly hope so. Thank you.'

'No problem,' he replied.

After that conversation, we made small talk for a while before he told me that he had to leave so he could make it to his final appointment of the day. Before he went, I offered him another biscuit, one for the road, which he accepted with glee. He didn't eat it straight away but opened his briefcase and put it inside, saving it for later, for when his belly rumbled.

With a feeling of trepidation, I closed the front door behind him.

I went into the bedroom to see what kind of state Sarah was in. She was beside herself with anger, barely able to get her words out at first, and then the screaming started.

I tried my level best to reason with her, telling her that what I had done was for her own good. It was meant to help her – it was because I cared. But she didn't see it that way. I stood in the doorway, frightened to go any closer. Her arms flailed the air as she hurled insults at me. She picked up the lamp from her bedside unit, ripped out the electrical cord, and then flung it at me. I managed to back out of the room just in time, using the door to protect myself. The lamp smashed against it and I felt the impact vibrating through the door handle. A tingling sensation raced up my fingers and then my arms as I gripped the handle defensively. I walked away and didn't re-enter the room for the rest of the day or night.

The couch would be my bed. As usual, I watched TV for a bit. Before I thought about sleeping, I got a bottle of red wine from the kitchen, uncorked it, and then drank it straight down. As I lay on the couch, I cradled the open bottle in my arms. It felt like a substitute for my son. This alcohol was my comfort, my baby. With the neck of the green bottle tilted against my chin, I began to feel weary. Without drinking much, I gave up on myself and fell asleep, fully clothed and fully beaten.

# he comes to me in dreams #2

I was back in the white world, standing there as I had before. This time my body was in full view right from the start. Directly in front of me was a child's swing; it was the only thing apart from myself that was visible. The frame was made from metal and the posts were sticking into the white ground, keeping it steady. The plastic seat rocked back and forth, indicating that someone had just been using it. It was unnerving. There was a particular eeriness about it. I walked over to the swing and put my hand on the seat to stop it from moving. When I did that, I heard the echo of a child's laughter. It was an evil sound, the sort of laugh you would hear on a ghost ride at the fairground, and the noise felt like it was surrounding me three hundred and sixty degrees.

I sat on the seat and listened to the laughter. It grew louder and louder. It got so loud that I had to cover my ears with my hands to try to protect them. I closed my eyes and tilted my head down towards the ground. With my hands still shielding my ears, I heard the noise begin to peak. It was so loud that I thought my head was going to explode. My ears were overpowered by a high-pitched ringing sound. Suddenly there was a gigantic bang. My heart raced like an Olympic sprinter's.

After the bang I sat for a few seconds, eyes still closed, too scared to open them. A short time later I opened my right eye and could see a cloud of white dust in front of me. I removed my hands from my ears, opening my left eye at the same time. There was a lot of dust in the air. I began to cough and choke as it filtered into my lungs, clogging them up. Waving my hands frantically, I tried to clear some of the dust particles from my face, allowing myself to breathe more freely. Within the cloud I saw a figure, the silhouette of a little boy. I stopped waving my arms and tried to focus on him as closely as I could. He smiled at me before inhaling a long deep breath. His cheeks puffed up and then he exhaled, blowing air in my direction. His exhalation wasn't normal but had the strength of a gale-force wind – so strong it made the swing rock backwards and forwards. I held on to the rope that connected the seat to the frame as tightly as I could. I swung so high that I was sure I'd fall off, but thankfully I didn't. Using all my strength, I somehow managed to hold on.

Everything settled. All the white dust had been blown away. As the swing slowed to a halt the boy was now clearly in view, standing in front of me. He looked to be possibly four years old, definitely no younger than that. He wore a pair of navy denim jeans and a red and royal-blue checked shirt. He smiled at me and spoke.

'Can I have a go on the swing, Daddy?'

My eyes filled up with tears of happiness. My heart fluttered.

'Of course you can, Son.'

I got off the seat and tried to pick him up. I moved my hands towards his armpits in order to lift him, but just before I could touch him something blocked me. I tried and tried again, but with the same result each time. It was as if there was an invisible shield guarding him, stopping me from making contact. Scared of forcing it too much, I let him get on the swing by himself. I was happy just to see him.

He used his feet to push himself off and swung peacefully back and forth. I sat on the white ground and watched him. With his cheeky child's smile, he continued swinging and started gathering momentum, picking up pace. He was having fun, and I enjoyed watching him.

'Daddy, Daddy, do you want to see me jump from the swing?' he asked.

'I would love to see you jump,' I replied. 'I'll count down from three, and when I get there, you jump, okay?'

He nodded and started swinging faster and higher.

'THREE, TWO, ONE, NOW JUMP!' I said excitedly.

Leaping from the seat, he flew through the air in front of me. It seemed like he was moving against the whiteness in slow motion, a smile still stretched across his face and his eyes sparkling. It was a moment of wonderment for him. He had reached a good height, but before he could start his descent he vanished. In the blink of an eye he disappeared. I got to my feet and ran in the direction he had jumped. There was nothing. He'd evaporated through some sort of white hole. I moved my hands about through the empty air and then over the white ground, trying to locate something. I was left disappointed.

Then an idea hit me. I would do what James had done. I sat on the swing, pushed myself off, and then picked up speed. I felt excited; I was sure this would work. As I had for James, I counted myself down from three and then jumped into the air. But unlike him, I plummeted to the ground, landing on my side, hurting my right wrist and winding myself in the process.

I lay there, unable to breathe, feeling dejected. The fairground laughter that I'd heard previously started up again. Why would my son be laughing at my pain? I asked myself. Maybe he didn't understand what was happening to me. Maybe none of this was even real. It was only a dream, after all.

With renewed determination, I got to my feet and returned to the swing for a second attempt. I thought that I had jumped too high and possibly missed the target James had hit. On my second attempt, I went slower and jumped less boldly, but this time I landed on my back. The laughter became louder and was beginning to upset me. One last time I tried. I pushed off, gathered as much pace as possible, and then strove for the greatest height I could reach. While in mid-flight, I thought this was it, I would really do it this time, but once again I crashed to the ground, breaking my fall with my already injured wrist. After that attempt, I didn't try again. I lay on my side, holding my hurt wrist in my other hand, listening to the eerie laughter echoing in the background. Tears welled up in my eyes. I closed them, and within my dream I lay down and fell asleep.

# rise and shine

When I woke up in the real world, I felt bad – dreadful actually. Although I hadn't had much to drink and was free from any sort of hangover, within myself I didn't feel right. The wine bottle that I'd been drinking from had fallen from my sleepy grasp, landing on our costly cream carpet. The majority of the remaining red wine had spilled from the bottle, leaving what looked like a small pool of blood staining the carpet. Moving on to my side, I reached down and felt the stain with my fingers. The wine had dried and penetrated deep into the fibre. It was going to be tough to remove, but I didn't really care about that.

With my right arm, I reached down and lifted the empty bottle off the floor. While doing so, I felt my wrist twinge, and I had to drop the bottle again as I winced with pain. I felt my right wrist with my left hand and it was throbbing. I tried rotating it in circles and then moving it in all different directions, but my movements were restricted to the bare minimum due to the pain. I thought about what could have caused my injury, but there was no obvious answer. There was only one thing going through my head: it was my dream. I had hurt my wrist in my dream.

'How can this be possible?' I asked myself aloud. 'Don't you start losing your fucking mind as well,' I added.

After debating my own sanity for a while, I settled on the more sensible conclusion that during the night I must have slept on it awkwardly, and that was that. It was the only reasonable answer I could come up with, so I had to accept it. The alternative was too difficult to contemplate.

I didn't want Sarah to see the mess that I'd made of the carpet. It would just give her more ammunition against me. So with my good arm I dragged the couch forward to cover the stain, and rearranged some of the other furniture so the couch didn't look strange or out of place. Fingers crossed, she wouldn't notice or question anything. She hardly left the bedroom anyway, and when she did she was oblivious to most things. She'd just drift in and out of the different rooms as if she were a ghost. I was quite confident that she wouldn't notice any of my forced feng shui. After, I went to the kitchen and saw the prescription the doctor had written out for her. It was on the table. I didn't want Sarah seeing that either, so I folded it in half and put it in my jeans pocket.

Too scared to go into the bedroom and change my clothes, I went to the bathroom instead, where I brushed my teeth and wet my hair. My hair was growing longer and scruffier with each stressful day that went by. It was the longest it had ever been, even in my younger, wilder days. As I looked in the mirror, something glinted, capturing my attention. I put my face up close to the mirror.

There was a solitary grey hair on the right-hand side of my head. It was one grey hair in amongst the thousands of black ones, but this one was standing to attention like a soldier saluting me; it was undeniable. I had no idea when it had appeared but it wasn't staying. I sifted through the surrounding hairs until I had that one grey traitor clamped between my index finger and thumb. I was ready to pull it right out of my scalp. But at the last second I changed my mind. If this was my inevitable future, was there any sense in fighting it? If this was the natural ageing process, if this was a mark of maturity, then why should I try to avoid it? So I left it in, certain there would soon be more on the way. I sprayed some deodorant into my armpits and tried to make myself look as presentable as I could before leaving the flat to go to the pharmacy.

Winter grabbed hold of me as I left the building. It was as if it had arms and legs and was wrapping itself around me. The chill was smothering, suffocating. It made my eyes widen and my skin shiver.

It was a short walk to the pharmacy. Where we lived, there was almost everything we needed right on our door-step. Although it was mid-morning, the sky was dark and overcast, a strong wind beginning to pick up. I walked briskly, hurried along by the forceful gusts pushing at my back. At the shop, apart from the two old female employees, I was the only one there. One of them was stacking shelves with assorted toiletries while the other was behind the counter, filling out paperwork. As I walked up to the counter, I removed my hands from my pockets, put them up to my mouth, and blew warm air into them, helping to defrost them. The lady behind the counter smiled and spoke.

'It really is winter now, isn't it?'

'You can say that again. I've only been outside for a few minutes and I'm freezing already.'

'You certainly look it. So, what can I do for you today, then?'

'I just need to hand in this prescription. It's for my wife. Is that okay?'

'Sure, let's have a look.'

I handed her the folded-up piece of paper. She had a pair of glasses hanging around her neck. She put them on, unfolded the prescription, and read it.

'Right, let's see if we have these in stock. I'll be back in a tick.'

I nodded. She disappeared into the back of the pharmacy for a few minutes. When she returned, her glasses hung around her neck again and she had a small box in her hand.

'Here we are. Has your wife ever taken anything like these before?'

'No. She doesn't like taking pills at all. She won't even take a paracetamol when she's got a headache. I think she prefers the suffering.'

'I see. There are a lot of people out there like that. Then, at the other end of the spectrum, there are people on all sorts of pills, some taking dozens each day just to get by.'

'Yeah, I guess there are.'

'She'll need to be careful with these ones, though. They're quite strong.'

'What are they?'

'Prozac. They're the most common type of antidepressant.'

'I know the ones.'

'You do?'

'Well, not from direct experience, but I've heard of them at least.'

'I see. Well, she should start by taking only one a day, and then build it up from there. You should probably get her to make another appointment with her GP in a month or so, just for a check-up to see if the pills are making any difference.'

'I'll get her to do that.' The pharmacist put the box into a white paper bag and handed it to me. 'Thanks,' I added.

The prescription was free. I was ready to leave.

'Oh, before you go, can I say one more thing?' the pharmacist jumped in. 'It's imperative she doesn't consume any alcohol while taking these. She won't get better if she mixes it with these drugs. I've seen it go wrong for people at first hand, believe me.'

That last sentence worried me. I wanted to ask some more about it, her own first-hand experience, but I was too polite for my own good to be intrusive.

'I'll take note of that. Thanks for all your help today,' was all I could muster up in return before leaving.

I stepped outside into the chill. I put my hands in my jacket pockets along with the white paper bag with the pills in it. The thought of returning to the flat straight away didn't appeal to me. Sarah might be awake and if so would most certainly still be fuming at me, so I decided to delay my return by going for a cup of coffee. At the end of the street, right on the corner, was a small Italian café, its windows fogged with condensation. I couldn't see anything properly through them, only a palette of muted colours. As I entered, my ears were overpowered by noise. The place was packed.

A loud, over-tanned authentic Italian lady took my order and then my money before handing me my coffee in a large cup. She didn't thank me, she didn't smile, she seemed devoid of basic manners, but that didn't bother me.

Coffee in hand, I found a table tucked away in a back corner. I sat down and took a few sips of my drink. It was strong, just how I liked it. With nothing else to do, I took the white paper bag from my pocket and examined the pills.

The information on the packaging wasn't very clear. I couldn't understand much of what it was supposed to be telling me, so I opened the box and took out the leaflet from inside. It contained a lot more information but the section that really caught my attention was the extensive list of side effects. These included: headaches, nausea, vomiting, anxiety, insomnia, dizziness, nervousness, diarrhoea, loss of appetite, sweating, and then out of nowhere, last but certainly not least, suicidal thoughts or behaviour. I presumed that the pharmaceutical companies noted such a long list of side effects in order to cover themselves in advance against any assertion whatsoever of harm suffered while taking the medication. Or maybe that was just my cynicism at work. I read the rest of the leaflet – front, back, and then the front again. By this point, I'd finished my coffee and it was time for me to leave. I got up from my chair, put the pills back in my jacket pocket and took my empty cup up to the counter. I handed it to the same hard-faced woman who'd served me, and she just about managed to crack a smile this time but still didn't thank me.

On my way back home, I walked past a florist's. A couple of paces beyond the entrance I stopped, turned around, went back and walked into the shop. Inside, the air felt wonderful: warm and fresh and alive. The vibrant blooms lit up the interior, turning it into a miniature oasis of colour in the grey wintry scene. A young couple were working there. I stood browsing the selection of flowers and out of the corner of my eye caught sight of the assistants kissing. It reminded me of how Sarah and I once were, reminded me of young love and expectation. I suppose most couples are like that at one time. Even the ones whose relationships end on the worst of terms must have felt like that in the beginning. It's amazing how things can change so dramatically. Maybe the couple in the florist's would be together forever and stay happy, or maybe theirs would turn out to be another story of lost love. I hoped they wouldn't end like that; they looked made for each other.

I reproached myself for nosiness and switched my attention back to the flowers. I had no idea which ones to buy. I'd only ever bought Sarah flowers as a gift on Valentine's Day, and I'd always gone for the predictably safe option of plain red roses. Hardly appropriate for this situation. As I struggled to make my choice, the male assistant, who looked slightly younger than me, came over.

'Can I help you with anything today?' he asked.

'Yeah, please. I could do with a lot of help actually.'

'Tell me, what kind of thing is it you're looking for?'

'I'm not sure. Something bright, I suppose. They're meant to help cheer someone up.'

'Are they for a female?'

'Yeah, they're for my wife.'

'Do you have any idea what type of flowers she likes?'

'Nope, none at all. I'm totally clueless.'

'Right then, let's see.'

He circled the tiny shop, narrowing down the options.

'I would go for these ones, I reckon,' he said, pointing to a large bunch of orange, yellow, pink and purple flowers. 'Yes, definitely these,' he added, as he skimmed the petals with his fingertips. 'They'll do the trick.'

'What kind are they?'

'They're a mixture of carnations, lilies, roses and chrysanthemums.'

'I'm not sure why I asked that actually. Makes no difference to me what they are. They look nice enough though, so I guess I'll just take them. As long as you think they're going to work.'

'I guarantee it,' he said with an air of breezy confidence.

'You can guarantee it?'

'Yeah, and if they don't work, come back and I'll give you something else free of charge. What do you say to that?'

'Deal. And I'm definitely going to hold you to that.' We both laughed.

He wrapped the arrangement in cellophane, put it in a gift bag, and then rang it through the till. The flowers cost a pretty penny, but hopefully they'd make Sarah smile.

The bouquet was so big that I had to use both hands to carry it. The flowers looked out of place in the bleak street outside the shop – an explosion of colour amidst the grey.

Before returning to the flat, I popped into the store to pick up a box of chocolates to go along with the flowers. I got dark ones; Sarah preferred dark chocolate to milk. I looped the handles of the carrier bag over my wrist. On the way home I found it hard to see what was in front of me as the big bunch of flowers blocked my view, but I managed to make it back to the flat without walking into anyone or anything. I tried to open the front door, but it was locked. Between the flowers and the carrier bag, it was a struggle to free my left hand in order to get the keys from my jeans pocket, but I managed it without dropping anything.

Inside, everything was as I'd left it. No noise, no movement, nothing. I went to the kitchen and put the flowers and chocolates on the unit. In the cupboard under the sink I found a glass vase, which I took out and filled with water. After removing the flowers from their wrapping, I untied and arranged them. I carried the vase full of beautiful colours towards the bedroom. I stood outside for a moment, listening for any sort of noise. Still nothing, so I opened the door and went in. Somehow, I'd forgotten about the lamp, the one Sarah had thrown at me. I took my first few steps into the room over broken pieces of the ceramic base. My footsteps crunched and crackled. The noise woke Sarah and she looked at me briefly before slithering back under the covers. I put the vase on the bedside unit and stood over her, waiting for her to acknowledge me.

The duvet rose and fell with each breath she took, but Sarah didn't come up for air. She stayed hidden from me.

'I got you some flowers,' I said. 'I hope they make you feel better. There are some chocolates too, dark ones. Would you like me to bring them through?'

There was no response. I retrieved a dustpan and brush from the kitchen and swept up the pieces of broken lamp. Then I left the bedroom, closing the door behind me. The rest of the afternoon passed uneventfully. I sat in the living room, watching TV. It was beginning to feel like my whole life revolved around watching that fucking TV. That was all I seemed to do: waste my time watching meaningless, idiotic crap. The realisation didn't stop me from watching more nonsensical programmes, though. I sat there and, for some reason, opened and ate the whole box of chocolates that I'd bought for Sarah.

When it got late I went to bed. Despite Sarah's difficult mood, I didn't want to spend another night on the couch. It was comfortable enough to sit on and for the occasional nap, but a whole night's sleep was a hard ask, let alone a series of nights. Anyway, it was as much my bed as it was Sarah's, so I crept into our room, got undressed, and carefully crawled into bed. Sarah was in a deep sleep and didn't notice me. In order not to wake her, I lay as still as possible and quickly drifted off.

There were no dreams that night – well, none that I could remember, at least. However, my deep sleep was interrupted. I could feel something happening to me. I opened my eyes. My bedside lamp was on. Sarah was on top of me, naked. She straddled me, moving urgently and panting with the effort. She must have removed my boxer shorts while I was sleeping. I didn't know what to make of her behaviour. We hadn't made love for months; we hadn't even spoken about it. Not that this was love as I remembered it, far from it, but if this was what it took to get my wife back, I was more than happy to go along with it.

As I lay there erect, she stared down at me. There was anger in her eyes. It wasn't a look I wanted to see, so I closed my eyes and thought about other times when we'd made love, times when it actually meant something, times when she looked sexy. While I was doing that, I felt something land on my face. I opened my eyes once more to see a rainbow of colour falling down on me. Still Sarah sat over me. She had the bouquet of flowers in her hands and was tearing them apart. Petals rained down on my shoulders, my face, my eyes. Some even fell into my gobsmacked mouth.

'What the hell are you doing?' I asked, spitting them out.

She began crying, and then started hitting my chest with the stripped wet stems until my skin turned red.

'Get the hell off me, right now!' I yelped.

She continued trying to have sex, which for me at least was now an impossibility. I put my hands on her shoulders and pushed her off me. She fell backwards on to the end of the bed. With the stems of the flowers still in her hand, she ran naked out of the room, roaring and bawling in a fit of hysteria and sudden realisation. The door banged shut behind her. In disbelief at what had just happened, I shook my head and got out of bed. I looked at the mess all around. The flowers that were meant to be a symbol of sympathy, understanding and love now lay in tatters on our deserted bed. I didn't know what to do.

# back to school

It was the first day of December. More notably, it was my first day back at work, my first day back at the school since James had died. I really dreaded it, but staying in the house, watching my wife's condition deteriorate further, wasn't helping my own battered self-esteem, and no matter how I tried, she wouldn't let me help her. There seemed no point in my staying with her only to be rejected, and someone had to keep the money coming in since there was no prospect of Sarah being fit for work.

When I woke up, I felt shattered. The anticipation of returning to the classroom had gotten the better of me, resulting in a shitty night's sleep. I crawled out of bed and forced myself under a cold shower. I hoped that the shock of the freezing water would jolt me awake. I achieved my goal only to feel nerves creep in as I dressed in my work clothes: dark jacket and cords, shirt and tie.

I sat in the kitchen and tried eating some cornflakes, but I was too nervous. Even a small bowl of cereal was too much for me to handle. Instead, I drank some black coffee. I sat staring at the clock, watching the hands tick round and round, praying for something to delay my inevitable and unavoidable return to work.

Sarah was still unaware of the pills the doctor had

prescribed for her. I thought about telling her, pleading with her to take them, if only for a short period of time. But there was no chance of that. Knowing that she wouldn't take them voluntarily, I devised a plan. Before I left the flat, I made her a strong cup of tea. I took a strip of the Prozac capsules out of the box and popped two of them from the foil-covered sleeve. With my fingers, I broke open the first capsule and poured the powdered contents into the tea. I did the same with the second capsule. I recalled the pharmacist telling me to start off slowly and then build it up from there, but it seemed to me that drastic measures were called for so I went in full steam ahead. I stirred the tea thoroughly and took a sip from the cup. It tasted just the same as it always did; there was no way she'd notice.

The only thing I needed now was for Sarah to drink it. I took the cup to the bedroom and placed it on the bedside unit. I kissed Sarah on the forehead and left the flat, hoping that she'd guzzle down every last bit of my sneaky cocktail and feel better for doing so. However devious it was of me, my plan was well-intentioned.

Outside, the temperature had plummeted further. My black car was silvered by a hard night frost. I tried to open the door but my hand stuck to the surface. The door wouldn't open; my hand wouldn't move. Eventually I wrenched it free, leaving a thin layer of skin from my palm attached to the handle. My hand burned and stung like crazy. Letting fly a few choice swear words, I walked around to the passenger side of the car. Fortunately, I managed to get that door to open, but not without a struggle.

Inside the cold car, I climbed awkwardly across the gear stick and handbrake to position myself in the driver's seat. I put the key in the ignition and turned it. With a cough and a splutter, the car started. There was no chance of going anywhere, though. The windscreen was covered in so much frost that I couldn't see anything. I put the heater on full, took a can of de-icer out of the glove compartment, and got back out of the car. It took me a good ten minutes to de-ice the vehicle and make it roadworthy. By then I was running late – not what I had wanted for my return to work.

Once finished, I got back inside the now warm interior and began the drive to school. Usually my journey there was accompanied by music on the radio, songs that I would sing along to, but that day I drove in silence, only the noise of traffic for a soundtrack. As I entered the school's car park, memories surfaced – of the day I'd received the phone call, the day I'd lost my son. Vivid, detailed flashbacks of that crushing time followed, and I couldn't shake them from my head.

I found a space and parked. I sat in the car, my legs shaking too much for me to get out. Pupils walked past. Some of them looked in on me as they strolled by at their leisurely pace, probably wondering what had happened to me and why I hadn't been there for a number of weeks. The thought of turning the engine back on and driving straight back out of the school gates was very appealing, but this was no time to be cowardly. I must get back to some sort of normality, even if I had to force myself. I waited for a gap in the oncoming crowds before making my escape from the car. Walking at my quickest pace and with my head tilted towards the ground, I made it to the school building and into the teachers' lounge without talking or making eye contact with anyone. It was a relief, but now there was another obstacle for me to face: the other teachers.

All eyes turned to me when I walked in. I acknowledged their pity, the commiserations murmured on every side, nodding my head and forcing a wry smile. I didn't say anything or engage directly with anyone but stayed silent. I went over to where the kettle and mugs were kept, flicked the switch. As I waited for the water to boil, I stared out of the window. A cloud of steam rose from the kettle, warming my face, clouding my vision. I wiped my eyes with my sleeve. Once I'd made my coffee I sat down with all the other teachers.

There were some strained exchanges. No one mentioned or asked about what had happened. I guess it was easier for everyone just to avoid the subject. Time ticked by. The other teachers started filing out, making their way to their respective classrooms to start the day. I stayed put until the very last moment, feeling safer between the four familiar walls. I didn't want to leave. Eventually, though, I had to.

My classroom was pretty much as I'd left it. I sat down at my desk and opened one of the drawers to put my things away. While doing so, something caught my eye. In the drawer was a photograph of Sarah and myself, taken when we were on our honeymoon only two years ago. We looked tanned and healthy, smiling and happy. We looked like we were in love. We didn't look like that anymore. Underneath the photograph was another picture, an ultrasound. I took it out of the drawer and observed it closely. If only we could go back to that time when we'd had so much to look forward to. My eyes welled up. I kissed the picture of our unborn baby, our now dead baby, before tucking it away at the very back of the drawer. Along with it, I stored my wallet, my keys and my phone. I placed them all on top of our honeymoon photo so that our smiling faces were covered. Then I closed the drawer.

With a bad feeling in my stomach and a swirling sensation in my head, I sat at my desk, waiting for the bell to ring. I could hear some of the pupils gathering on the other side of the door, also waiting for the bell to sound. And then it came. The noise made me shudder.

What I'd dreaded for weeks was now imminent. The door opened and a sea of obnoxious, smart-arse adolescents filtered noisily into the room and took their seats. Since I was a maths teacher and this was a maths lesson, the pupils lined their desks with various objects they thought they might require. Out came jotters, calculators, pens, pencils, rulers and other assorted stationery. They were all much more prepared than I was. I tried hard to hide my nerves from them. After all, I was the only adult in the room. They should be intimidated by me, not the other way around.

Once everyone was seated and quiet, I tried to get on with the lesson in hand. It was a struggle. My voice trembled as I spoke. I heard it myself. My mouth was dry. I went to take a drink of water but my hand shook as I lifted the glass to my mouth. The whole class witnessed it. I studied them. Their reactions were mixed. Some of the kinder pupils looked concerned and sympathetic. Those at the other end of the scale, the troublemakers, stared at me with spite in their eyes, as if I deserved every minute of what I was going through, as if this was payback for something I had done to them. I tried to ignore what was happening, but it was impossible.

With great difficulty I struggled through two classes without any major breakdowns. But the third and final class before lunch would be my biggest challenge.

These pupils were older. When they entered, the males swaggered in with their stupid haircuts and their scruffy looks. They'd left the top buttons of their shirts undone, and their black and white striped ties were loosely knotted. Their trousers hung low, and their rucksacks bounced off the base of their spines with every step they took. They stomped their way over to their seats, pushing and shoving each other, ignoring their teacher. The females glided in behind them. Their black skirts were short, revealing too much skin for their pubescent male counterparts to look at without feeling giddy. The girls' bras were pushed up high in an attempt to convey the impression that they were the owners of large voluptuous breasts, which the males fell for hands down. For the girls, the entrance to the classroom was more like walking down a catwalk than coming to a lesson.

There didn't seem to be much interest in the learning aspect of the class, apart from among the small minority who actually cared about their futures. I sat at my desk, waiting patiently for everyone to settle. Eventually they did. I spotted an empty seat at the back of the room. I got up from my chair, stood worriedly in front of the intimidating teens, and began the lesson.

After stuttering through a few questions that I read from a textbook, I heard a knock on the door.

'Come in,' I said.

The door slowly opened and my worst nightmare entered the room. His name was Kyle, and he was a cunt for someone so young. He had bleached-blonde sections through his hair, which was sprayed and gelled into a Mohican. His face was red and spotty, wearing an evil grin. I was surprised that someone like him had lasted so long in the educational system. There was no apology for being late; he just sauntered by me as if I wasn't even there. He stank of cigarette smoke.

'Welcome back, sir,' he said to me over his shoulder.

His rudeness and sarcasm were infuriating. Right there and then, in front of the whole class, I wanted to beat the living shit out of him. At his own leisurely pace, he got to his desk and sat down. Noisily, he took things out from his backpack and slammed them down on the desk with brute force, for the sole purpose of causing further disruption to the lesson. I stood there, glaring at him. All I wanted was for him to stop. I could feel my face boiling up, turning red, veins popping. My patience was rapidly escaping me. I tried ignoring him the best that I could and continued with the lesson in hand.

When I spoke to the class, I spoke as loudly as I could, trying to hide my nervousness. Between my sentences, I could hear Kyle chatting to one of his friends who was stationed at the desk behind him. Kyle wasn't facing me. All I could see was the back of his head and that stupid crested hair of his. I wanted desperately to say something, but I didn't have the confidence to speak up, so I let it go. If he didn't want to learn and improve himself as a person, that was his loss. I stood in front of the class, all eyes fixed on me, like I was on trial for murder. My voice began to tremble even more. My mouth was now bone dry. Shakily, I made my way back to my desk, took a sip of water, and tried to compose myself. It didn't work. My legs nearly gave way, so I sat down. I looked up and every single eye was trained on me apart from Kyle's and his mate's.

They were still chatting away, oblivious to anything

I was doing. The rest of us sat in silence. Kyle's words seemed to resonate louder and louder. It was as if he was shouting them straight into my ear and they were rattling through my brain. I could feel my rage building and building, and then it peaked.

'GET THE FUCK OUT OF HERE, YOU LITTLE PRICK! YOU'RE MEANT TO RESPECT ME, YOU FUCKING PIECE OF SHIT!' I yelled at the top of my voice.

That wild outburst finally caught his attention. He stopped talking and turned to look at me.

'YES, I'M TALKING TO YOU, KYLE!'

Extending my left arm, I pointed at him with my index finger.

'YOU'RE A LITTLE CUNT! I WANT YOU TO GET YOUR THINGS TOGETHER AND GET THE HELL OUT OF HERE, RIGHT NOW!'

He sat still and stared at me, in shock, along with the rest of the stunned class. I'd given him a chance, but still he didn't move. Eventually he did something that sent me further over the edge. As I stared at him wild-eyed, his expression changed. It broke into that familiar cheeky grin of his, and I went crazy at the sight of it. I stormed up to his desk, grabbed him by the shoulders of his thick, black school blazer, and pulled him out of his chair. He was on the floor, squirming, that evil grin of his completely wiped away. Now, he looked like a little boy, but that look of innocence didn't stop me from doing what I did next. I grabbed him by the collar of his shirt and dragged him across the floor until we reached the classroom door. He kicked his feet and tried to loosen my grip with both of his hands, but I was too strong for him. When we got to the door, I lifted him to his feet and pushed him out into the hallway.

'GET THE HELL AWAY FROM ME!'

As I shouted, spittle sprayed from my mouth, landing on his blazer. He looked straight at me – first in disbelief, and then with uncertainty as to what his next move should be. I could have sworn his eyes were watering. And then he spoke in an ever so soft voice.

'I'm sorry,' he said, very quietly. 'I'm really sorry.'

I shook my head and laughed out loud.

'What about my things?' he asked.

I thundered my way back to his desk, shoved his possessions into his rucksack and took them out to the hallway. I didn't say anything but threw the rucksack towards his face. Luckily for him he had good reflexes. We exchanged one last long glance before I slammed the classroom door in his face.

Kyle was gone and it was a relief not to see his hateful features anymore. I felt exhausted. My eyelids were too heavy to stay open. I leaned forward, resting my forehead against the door, and took in deep breaths. I had forgotten about the rest of the class. When I eventually straightened up and turned around, I took in their expressions of horror and amazement.

'WHAT?' I shouted. 'IN FACT, EVERYONE CAN GO. YOU CAN ALL LEAVE. GET YOUR THINGS TOGETHER AND GET OUT OF HERE RIGHT THIS SECOND!'

There was no hesitation. No one dithered or dallied, understandably. No one else wanted to be dragged across the cold hard floor like Kyle had been. I opened the door again and stood by it as the pupils quickly filed out of the classroom. Not one of them muttered a word, either to me or to each other. Not one of them made eye contact or even looked at me. They were all too scared. It was a case of heads down and get out of there as quickly as possible without any further incidents. They were soon gone.

I closed the door behind them but could hear some of them talking about me in the hallway. Words like 'psychopath' and 'freak' were being bandied about with worrying regularity before the voices faded away. I was now alone in my empty classroom, worn out after all the drama. I walked back to my desk and opened the drawer. I took out the picture of the ultrasound scan, placed it on the desk, and stared at it. My eyes began to close – I couldn't stop them, so I rested my head on top of the desk and fell asleep.

## he comes to me in dreams #3

Back again. Back in the familiar white scenario of my dreams, although this time the setting was quite different. It wasn't anywhere near as sparse as on my previous visits. My whole classroom was there, laid out in the empty space. All the desks and chairs were arranged in just the same way. I was sitting at my desk. It was only when I tried moving that I realised something was wrong. My arms and legs were chained to the four stumpy wooden legs of the desk. The chain links were thick and heavy, and they shone. I tugged on them hard to see whether there was any chance of wrenching myself free, but it wasn't worth the effort. They were far too heavy for my puny limbs so I just sat there with nothing to do. I looked around the classroom and noticed something strange, something different. Way beyond the last row of desks, a long way into the distance, stood a black door. It was alone and unsupported, attached to nothing. I sat patiently, unsure of where the dream was going. There didn't seem to be any plot to this one. I knew that black door would have some part to play, though. It had to or it wouldn't be there. It had to be of some significance.

After a long wait, my hunch proved to be right. The black door creaked open, allowing a flash of heavenly white light to shine through. Startled, I lifted my chained wrists to my face to stop the light from blinding me. The door quickly shut and the light disappeared. I took my hands away from my eyes, able to see again. A teenaged boy was standing there in front of the black door. He was dressed in full school uniform, the uniform of the school where I taught, and he had a rucksack over his shoulders. He looked a bit shy, but smart and well presented. With slow steps he walked towards the desks and stopped at the first one he reached. It was in the back row, farthest away from me. Removing his rucksack, he sat down. He brought out a pencil and jotter and placed them on the desk. He opened the jotter and I saw straight away that he was left-handed, just like me. By the way that his left arm was moving, I could tell that he was drawing a picture rather than writing words.

Every so often, he would lift the jotter up in front of his eyes, turning it in different directions, inspecting his work in progress, viewing it from different angles, and then he'd put it back down and resume his work.

I enjoyed seeing him lost in concentration. I didn't want to spoil it by speaking. After some time he stopped what he was doing, put down his pencil and closed the jotter. With nothing else to do, he lifted his head and stared towards the front of my makeshift classroom. His eyes met mine. He smiled. I smiled back. The black door in the distance creaked open and a searing flash of light burst into the room once again. I was caught off guard this time and blinded by the light. The door closed and my hazy eyesight returned to normal.

Now I could see two people at a distance from me. The boy was standing and next to him was a woman, her back turned to me. She was fussing over him, adjusting his school tie, brushing back his hair, pinching his cheeks. The boy turned around. Both with their backs to me, they started walking towards the black door, hand in hand. As they walked, the woman swung round her head and looked at me over her shoulder. My heart skipped a beat and then stopped momentarily. It was Sarah, hand in hand with the boy who must be James.

I stood up and tried moving. The chains were long enough for me to get out of my chair and walk a few feet beyond the desk, but I was prevented from going further. It felt like walking into a brick wall. The closer they got to the door, the more determined I was to free myself. Feeling powerful and strong, I pulled on the chains and kicked out with my feet repeatedly until, with one thunderous blow from each leg, the chains snapped. I broke free from the desk, which shattered under the strain.

I tried to walk, but my wrists were still secured to the remnants of the desk. I only managed a short distance before I was forced to give up. Meanwhile, Sarah and James were drawing further away from me. With every last bit of energy and determination that I was able to conjure up, I threw my arms into the air and let out a scream. I felt like Bruce Banner when he morphed into the Incredible Hulk.

I felt unstoppable. The chains securing my wrists broke free and flew into the air. I was no longer restricted. I ran sluggishly towards the black door. My arms and legs ached. It felt like they were on fire. Despite the pain, I dragged myself on. By the end, I was on my hands and knees, crawling. Sarah and James had reached the door, and she turned her head around one final time to blow me a kiss. They walked into the light, closing the door behind them.

Sarah and James were gone, but I continued to crawl after them. I was like an injured bug. I reached the last desk, the one that James had sat at. I managed to haul my dead weight up from the floor to sit on his chair. His pencil and jotter were still on the desk. His jotter had his name written on the front. Opening it, I flicked through the pages. They were all blank, but then I came to one page that wasn't. It was the perfect page. A drawing – well, it was more of a doodle, but the subject made me happy. It was of the three of us, Sarah, James and me, all standing in a line, holding hands. After analysing each detail that he'd drawn, memorising it, I got to my feet, walked to the black door and grabbed the handle. Expecting to see the same blinding white light, I braced myself and covered my eyes, but it didn't come. Through the door, in the space beyond, was nothing but blackness. I took one tentative step forward, followed by another, and then another, until I was fully immersed in the darkness. I was unable to see anything, but I could hear a loud ringing sound.

# we need to have a little chat

It was the school bell that woke me. It was lunchtime. I'd only been asleep for the remainder of the last lesson, about forty minutes or so. Over the lunch period I didn't leave the classroom. I was too scared to, in case I bumped into any of the pupils who had witnessed my outburst or any of the other teachers who might have heard about it. I just sat at my desk and daydreamed. I didn't eat anything. When the second bell rang to indicate the end of lunch, I waited anxiously for my next class to arrive, but they didn't show. I could hear lots of people in the hallway, shuffling their feet and chattering, but they soon disappeared into all the other classrooms. All but mine. My initial thought was that I hadn't read my timetable correctly. I took it out and checked it, and then double-checked. I rubbed my eyes, in case I wasn't reading it properly, but I was definitely supposed to be teaching another lesson. Ten minutes went by and still no one showed. Then I heard footsteps, a heavy, purposeful tread, coming towards my classroom. There was a sharp knock on the door, and my boss entered.

'Mark, I think we need to have a little chat. Do you mind if I take a seat?'

'No, not at all. Go ahead.'

He pulled one of the classroom chairs over and set it down by my desk.

'I've just spent the last half-hour or so talking with Kyle McGuire. He was very distressed. He told me in great detail what you supposedly did to him. Tell me it's not true, Mark. Tell me he's lying, please.'

'I'm afraid I can't do that, George.'

'For fuck's sake, Mark!'

My boss didn't swear very often, so when I heard that, I knew things were bad.

'I don't know what happened to me. I just lost it. He was late for class and when he came in, he had that look on his face – that fucking smug look of his. Then he kept on chatting to one of the other pupils and wouldn't shut up. He was winding me up on purpose, I know he was. He pushed and pushed, trying to send me over the edge, and eventually he succeeded. He sent me way over the edge and beyond.'

'Jesus Christ, Mark! Did you actually pull him out of his chair and drag him across the floor, in front of the whole class?'

'Yes, unfortunately, I did.'

I put my hands to my head. I felt ashamed of my own actions, though a glimmer of satisfaction lurked unacknowledged as well. It was about time someone taught that little dickhead a lesson, put him in his place.

'Mark, you know I should probably sack you for what you did. You know that, right?'

'I know. I'm sorry, George.'

'I understand that you've been under a lot of stress recently and things have been hard for you, but you can't go around doing crazy stuff like that, especially not to pupils.'

'I know I can't.'

In that moment I felt like a child again, receiving a telling-off from my father. I hadn't been talked down to in this way for a long time.

'Well, listen. I spoke to Kyle, and I told him about what's been happening in your life ... that you haven't been well. I told him that he didn't have to take things any further, and he's happy to leave them as they are, but you'll need to apologise for what you did.'

'Sorry, run that by me again. You just said that you'd told him about what's been happening in my life. What the hell did you tell him exactly?' I asked, the tone of my voice changing from regretful to angry.

'I told him about Sarah, and the baby, and your loss.'

'You told him *what*?'

'I had to. If I hadn't explained then he'd more than likely have gone and complained to the school board, or the newspapers, or even the police. Then you'd be out of a job and quite possibly done for assault.'

'I don't want him knowing anything about my personal life! Now he'll have more ammunition to use against me. I can't believe you told him about my personal affairs!'

'Your actions left me no choice, Mark. You brought this on yourself. I was merely trying to save you your job, your career.'

'Fuck that!'

'Please, watch your language, Mark.'

'What else do you expect me to say?'

'I expect you to say thank you at the very least. I know things have been hard recently but—'

'THANK YOU!' I butted in, stopping him mid-sentence.

I couldn't quite comprehend the garbage that was coming out of his mouth. He was taking sides with that little bastard Kyle!

'I've just saved your job for you, and I really didn't have to,' George reproached me.

'That little piece of shit deserved the beating of his life. He's a piece of crap, and you know it.'

'I know it, you know it, all the teachers in the school know it, but you can't go throwing pupils around the classroom just because you don't like them or because they've been winding you up. You should have put him on detention, punished him in the accepted way.'

'Detention is no fucking deterrent to hoodlums like him.'

'Well, that's the only option we've got, so we need to use it.'

'And you actually want me to apologise to him too?'

'Yes, you have to. Kyle requested one, face-to-face.'

'And if I don't?'

'Then he may take further action against you and you'd almost certainly lose your job. After all, he's got a whole classroom full of witnesses.'

'I can't apologise to him. He doesn't deserve it.'

'What are you saying?'

'I think it's obvious what I'm saying. I'm not going to do it. I refuse!'

'Don't be stupid. Just swallow your pride. It'll only take a minute or so. That's all he wants.'

'I can't do it. I won't do it.'

'Come on, Mark. Stop being so unreasonable. He's given you a way out of this.'

'Oh, yeah, he's such a kind, giving person. Well, I'll tell you what you can do. You can tell Kyle to shove his apology up his arse!'

I took my possessions from my drawer, including the photo of Sarah and me and the ultrasound scan of James, then got to my feet and put my jacket on.

'Where are you going?' George asked.

'Home.'

'Mark!' he shouted. 'If you leave now, you can't come back. You understand that, don't you?'

'I do, and I don't give a rat's ass! Just tell Kyle to fuck off!' I said, and began walking away.

'Don't be such a stubborn prick, Mark.'

I turned around, looked at the rector, resisting the temptation to go back and punch him in his round, chubby face.

'George, I know you're a good man, but I can't do what you're asking me to do, and I certainly don't appreciate you telling people about my personal affairs, especially not a pupil.'

'I had to, Mark. You need to understand that. You left me no choice.'

'And you need to understand that you can fuck off as well! I'm done with this place. Goodbye.'

That was the end of my teaching career. However, I like to think that I went out on a high, that my departure will be remembered. Certainly the stand I'd taken against Kyle remains one of my happiest memories. As I walked back to my car, I followed the same route as on that fateful day when I'd received the desperate phone call from Sarah. The moment of déjà vu sent shivers through my body and awoke other unwanted memories. I turned the engine on and drove out of the school gates without looking back. Good riddance to the place.

When I arrived back, in the early afternoon, Sarah was still in bed, the sheets pulled over her head. She didn't ask why I was home so early, and in the days that followed she didn't question why I was skulking around the house. She probably didn't notice I was there.

# put your pencil down

Days went by, lazy days. One morning, though, I got up and decided to force myself out of the slump that I'd found myself trapped in. It was the start of a new day. I was feeling fresh and energetic for once. I set myself up for the change of pace ahead by cooking a hearty fried breakfast. I had the complete works – sausages, bacon, eggs, beans, mushrooms, toast – washing it all down with a pint of fresh orange juice without bits. It went down well. To cleanse myself of the grease-ridden but mightily enjoyable meal, I took a shower. Once dried, I changed into some smart clothes – well, smart in comparison to the joggers and T-shirt combination I'd been hanging about in. After that, I continued my transformation by doing some housework. The flat hadn't been cleaned or even touched since the whole sorry saga of losing James began. I tackled every room. I vacuumed the carpets, mopped the kitchen floor, polished the tables, dusted the cabinets and the other furniture. I even cleaned the windows. I did everything with the exception of the bedroom in which Sarah was still stewing. I didn't dare disturb her.

After resting on the couch for half an hour, I got myself up and made my way to the newsagent's. I picked up a newspaper, one that was full of job vacancies, and for some bizarre reason decided to buy a pad of blank paper and a packet of six HB pencils, the ones with rubbers on the top. Back at the flat I sat in the kitchen, made myself a cup of coffee, and then looked through the paper. I waited for a vacant position to jump out at me, but none did. Nothing caught my attention. They were mostly office jobs, nothing with variety or value, nothing that would help improve the world.

I set the newspaper to one side and took out the packet of pencils and the pad of paper that I'd bought. I began sketching. For a while I doodled, drawing random objects. Then I stopped. My mind cleared and focused. I knew what I wanted to draw: the same picture that James had produced in my dream. I closed my eyes and tried to envisage every detail. I sought to re-create it on the blank page, details appearing to me in flashes, but I couldn't get it right. My drawing wasn't the same. I tried again and again, without stopping.

I'd gone through one pencil already, as well as numerous sheets of paper. We didn't have a pencil sharpener in the flat, which meant that when the lead of one became blunt, I ditched it for a fresh one from the pack. On my first effort, I spent thirty minutes trying to replicate James's creation, but to no avail. The following efforts were rushed, the quality steadily worsening. I wanted to see his drawing again, not just through the visions in my head but on paper. I wanted it to be real. I wanted to touch it. I wanted it so badly.

The kitchen floor that I'd mopped earlier in the day was no longer pristine. It now had a layer of crumpled-up paper scattered across it, pages of my poor artwork.

The afternoon slipped away from me. The clock read 5 p.m. I'd been drawing for well over an hour and hadn't come close to a match, not once. To ease my frustration, I took out a bottle of red wine and poured myself a glass. Tilting my chair back, I rested my head against the kitchen wall. With my eyes closed, I took occasional sips of wine.

Two glasses later, I felt ready to try again. I cracked my knuckles, stretched out my arms, and with a new pencil in hand I began another drawing. I put down each line with care. I didn't rush it like I had the previous attempts. Concentration was key. I kept my head down close to the paper, just to the right-hand side of the pad, and as I sketched with my left hand, my eyes examined every stroke I made with the pencil. My face was close to the table, so close in fact that my nose would occasionally brush the surface of it and I'd breathe in the fumes of the furniture polish that I'd applied to the wood earlier that morning.

I thought this attempt would be the one. I'd taken over half an hour to complete the drawing and was excited when I thought I'd done it. With my head lifted from the table, I set the pencil down and tore the sheet of paper from the pad. With trepidation, I viewed the drawing. On first inspection, I thought I'd achieved it. Line for line,

I was sure I'd matched the dream drawing. I felt a real sense of achievement. To be sure, though, I closed my eyes and cast my mind back to James's original sketch. In my head, I went through his drawing, recalling each line from start to finish, and when I opened my eyes I expected to see the exact same thing on the piece of paper before me. I didn't. Again, I was nowhere near, and in a fit of despondency I snapped the pencil in half and tore the sheet of paper into hundreds of little pieces. I threw them into the air above my head and tiny bits of paper fell down on me like a snowfall. With bits of the fake snow scattered through my hair, I sat there, disgusted and pissed off at myself.

It seemed to me that slow and steady was no longer the way to go. That tactic obviously wasn't working, and I'd lost all patience with it. The wine was flowing freely down my gullet and the drawings were coming thick and fast. I decided not to inspect each one. Instead I would just draw, set them to one side, and then view them once I'd run out of gas.

There was a stack of artwork piling up on the table. Time was running away from me and I wasn't up for the chase. Soon the wine had dried up so I went in search of whatever alcohol was available to me. Gin was the answer, Bombay Sapphire to be precise. Now all I needed was a mixer. When I took gin, which wasn't very often, I'd usually have it with tonic water; there was nothing like that in the flat. The only thing we had was cola. To my relief, it was drinkable, and the more I drank, the more palatable it became. This was probably due to my turning from tipsy to full-on drunk.

The alcohol gave me energy and self-belief. Without realising it, I'd produced over a hundred drawings and was down to the last few remaining sheets of paper. I felt exhausted and had a crippling cramp in my hand. I didn't try too hard on the final drawings. Surely I'd done enough. Surely one of my efforts in amongst the hundred or so would be the one.

I put my pencil down. It was time to judge what I'd done. Trembling with excitement, I picked up my stack of drawings and scrolled through them one by one, expecting to see a duplicate of what James had done. But with each drawing I looked at, my hopes diminished a little more. They were terrible, really terrible. I'd finished looking through the whole stack and not one of them was even close enough for me to pretend it was the same. I felt angry, but was too tired to express it adequately.

I got up and took the stack of paper over to the kitchen sink. I dried the sink with a tea towel, removing all moisture from it before placing the paper into it. Taking the top sheet from the pile, I lit it over a gas burner and used it to set fire to the rest of the stack in the sink. I watched as a gentle blue flame flickered and then spread across the pages. Shortly afterwards, a full-blown fire had broken out. The single flickering blue flame had turned into a gang of wicked red ones. They burned with a ferocious light. They looked hungry. I stood there, transfixed. Heat from the flames fanned my face. I had to shift my gaze from the brightness.

The paper quivered and wilted and flew around the sink as if looking for a way out. I could see individual lines being cremated, turning into black dust. Fragments escaped from the fire and floated in the air above the sink, like a swarm of bees. My whole day's work was disappearing before my eyes, and I couldn't be happier about it.

* * *

The next morning I found myself lying on the cold lino of the kitchen floor. A strong smell of smoke filled both the room and my lungs. I quickly got to my feet to inspect the remains of the fire. Luckily, it had died out. All that remained in the sink was a pile of black ash. Not one of the drawings had survived. Somehow, I must have fallen asleep as I stared at the glowing flames. I was relieved that I hadn't burned the whole flat down.

I turned on both the taps, hot and cold. Ash swirled around the sink before disappearing down the plughole. Once it was clear, I washed my hands. To disguise the smell, I sprayed copious amounts of air freshener throughout the kitchen. While I was doing this, I noticed that the gas burner was still lit. This frightened me. I turned it off immediately and opened the kitchen window. How could I have been such an idiot? I opened more windows throughout the flat, to get rid of the smell of burning and any harmful toxins polluting the air. The incoming breeze turned the cold flat even colder, but it had to be done.

My next task was to clean the kitchen again, the way I had the previous morning. Armed with a mop and bucket, I restored the place to showroom condition then retired to the bedroom for a proper sleep. Sarah didn't stir. I hoped that when she woke she wouldn't be able to tell that anything was wrong.

# a sad kitten

Days drifted by with nothing of real importance occurring. I slouched around in various rooms of the flat while Sarah continued to hide out in the bedroom. Then one day as I lay on the couch in the living room, I heard a scratching noise coming from the front door. It reminded me of chalk being run down a blackboard, not that modern schools actually use those anymore. I sat there, too lazy to get up and investigate. It would pass in its own time. It continued, and only stopped when I heard the front door opening. With that surprise, I bounced up from the couch and rushed through to the hallway.

Sarah was standing by the open door, wearing only a black bra and pants, nothing more. Her once sexy body had changed drastically over the past weeks. She'd lost a lot of weight, too much, and probably bordered on anorexic. Her ribcage poked out through pale, dirty-looking skin. The sight made me feel ill. She didn't seem to notice me standing in the hallway. She was staring at something on the floor, something that was stepping inside the flat.

It was a cat, a skinny, bedraggled one. It was shivering and looked sad. Just like Sarah. Its fur was white with patches of ginger, which didn't disguise the dirt that streaked it. The cat walked up to me, lifted its head and looked at me. After inspecting me for a few seconds, it promptly turned around and walked back to Sarah. It circled her legs, rubbing its back against her ankles. Sarah smiled and bent down to pick it up.

'What are you doing?' I asked, rushing over and managing to stop her.

'I was going to hold it.'

'You can't touch that thing.'

'Why not, exactly?'

'Just look at the state of it.'

'What? What's wrong with it?'

'It's dirty. A real mess. It's probably carrying all sorts of disease. Parasites … who knows what else.'

'No, it isn't.'

'Anyway, it probably belongs to someone.'

'Maybe. Or it could be a stray.'

'I doubt it. It's wearing a collar. It's a pet. For all we know, it could belong to one of the neighbours. There may be people out there looking for it right now.'

'I know, but look at the poor little thing. You said it yourself – whoever's been looking after it, they haven't been doing a good job. They obviously don't care about it.'

Sarah reached down and stroked the cat's head. It let out a loud purr.

'I suppose that's true.'

'Well?'

'Well, you can't keep it. It can't live here.'

'I know that, but it'll probably freeze to death if it stays outside much longer. Why don't we just keep it for the night? We can clean it up, give it a good scrub. And then after that we can give it a proper meal, and come tomorrow we'll let it out again. Then maybe it will go back to where it came from.'

'I'm not sure about this, Sarah.'

'Please, Mark. Please!'

Her hands were clasped together as if she was begging me. I had no choice but to agree.

'Okay, fine. But before you go touching it, you'll need to put on some proper clothes. You don't know what that cat might have.'

'Thanks, Mark.'

'No problem.'

'What do you think we should call him?' Sarah asked.

'So it's a male then?'

'Yeah, I think so. Don't you? What should we call him?'

'I don't know. You can decide, I guess.'

'George. Let's call him George.'

'Really, you think George?'

'Why? What's wrong with that?'

'I don't know. He just looks a bit too young for it. George sounds like an old person's name. Plus, it's the name of my ex-boss.'

Despite my saying that, Sarah still didn't ask about what had happened to me and my job. She bypassed it completely, too engrossed in paying attention to the furry intruder.

'Well, what about Jacob then? What about calling him that?'

'Jacob, yeah, that's better. I like Jacob.'

'Jacob it is then.'

For the first time in too long, I caught a glimpse of the Sarah I recognised. The way she cared so intensely about this unknown feline that had suddenly walked into our lives gave me a glimmer of hope – the old Sarah still lived, the one I hadn't seen for ages, the one who once loved me.

She ran to the bedroom, quickly threw on some clothes, and returned to me in the hallway. She picked up the scruffy-looking cat and took him to the bathroom. I went with her. She placed him in the bathtub and turned the taps on. I looked at her and laughed.

'What's so funny?' she asked.

'You can't put him in there! You'll drown the poor bugger.'

I turned the taps off and moved over to the sink, which I began filling with a mixture of hot and cold water. I felt it with my hand, testing the temperature. It was just right. I lifted the cat out of the tub and put him into the sink. The newly named Jacob twice tried to escape; eventually, though, he accepted his fate and began to enjoy the warmth of the water.

Sarah took a sponge from the side of the bathtub. She plunged it deep into the sink before squeezing it out over

Jacob's head. She grinned; he purred. She did it again, receiving the same response. As she bathed the cat I stood and watched. I put my hand on her shoulder, expecting her to flinch or make a barbed comment, but she didn't do either. She allowed my hand to stay there. It felt like a breakthrough.

We stayed in the bathroom for a while, messing around with Jacob. Once we'd all had enough and he was clean, Sarah wrapped him in a towel and took him through to the living room. The way she carried him was a bit disturbing. Like a baby.

I went to the kitchen and rummaged through the fridge, looking for any food that a cat might like. There was a packet of wafer-thin chicken slices, the kind designed for filling sandwiches. I took the packet out. I also filled a bowl with milk and set it down on the carpet in the living room.

Sarah lay on the floor, on her back, while Jacob walked around her. She sat up and I crouched beside her, holding the packet of chicken in my hand. One by one, we fed Jacob the slices. He ate them so fast that he eventually had to pause for breath. You could tell he hadn't eaten anything for days. He must have been scavenging bins, searching for roadkill, with little success.

Once he'd eaten all the chicken, he made his way to the bowl of milk and lapped at it. His tongue moved in and out of his mouth constantly. He didn't take a break, and it wasn't long before the bowl was empty and the only thing he was licking was the bottom of the bowl itself. I took it back to the kitchen, filling it with more milk. When I returned to the living room, Sarah was asleep on the couch, with Jacob napping on top of her. They looked happy like that so I didn't wake them. Instead, I put the bowl down on the carpet and sat in the other chair. I turned on the TV, keeping the sound muted, watching programmes with subtitles for the rest of the day.

* * *

Hours later, I heard a yawn from Sarah. She stretched her arms out wide, and opened her sleepy eyes. She smiled down at Jacob and ran her hand down his back, which in turn woke him. It was obvious that they were now good friends, two lost souls who had managed to find each other and were happy that they had.

The day flitted away from us quickly. Sarah and I had conversations, proper ones. We finally spoke about the school and what had happened there. I told her my plans for the future. When she asked questions, she did so with real interest, real care. She offered sensible suggestions, trying to help. And for the first time in weeks she ate a proper meal.

We retired to bed early that night, and we did so together. Sarah suggested that Jacob should accompany us and sleep at the foot of the bed. I wasn't overly keen on the idea, but was easily won over when she looked at me with her green eyes full of appeal. We climbed into bed and huddled together under the cold sheets. To get warm we held each other, while Jacob lay obediently at the bottom of the bed, curled up into a ball on top of the covers.

We snuggled, and despite her physical deterioration, her skin was as soft as ever. I held Sarah tightly in my arms. It felt like I finally had her back, and I didn't want to let go. As I drifted off to sleep, I thought about the future. How we might actually have one again. I fell asleep with a smile on my face and the woman I loved in my arms.

* * *

Shrieks and screams broke my dreams of happiness. They were coming from one of the other rooms, though I couldn't tell which one. I ran out into the hallway in my boxer shorts. Out of the corner of my eye, I caught a glimpse of Sarah. She was in the living room on her hands and knees. Her face was red. She was sobbing and punching the floor with her bony fists.

'Sarah, what's wrong?' I asked.

'It's Jacob. He's gone!'

'Gone where?'

'I don't know, but he's gone. He's not here.'

'Are you sure?'

'Yes, positive.'

'Are you sure he's not just hiding somewhere?'

'I've searched everywhere. He's definitely gone.'

'But that's not possible. The bedroom door was shut all night, and so was the window. How could he have gotten out?'

'How am I supposed to know?'

'It doesn't make sense. He couldn't just vanish.'

'Not unless someone opened the door in the middle of the night and shooed him out.'

She shot me an accusing look.

'What are you implying, Sarah?'

'I don't know.'

'Are you saying I did this? That I let him out deliberately?' I asked in disbelief.

'All I'm saying is, you didn't want Jacob here in the first place, and I wouldn't put it past you to do something devious like this.'

'Sarah, you're out of your mind! You truly have lost it.'

'Shut up, Mark!'

'You're right on one thing though.'

'What's that?'

'Yes, at first, I didn't want some disease-ridden stray cat living in our home. But when I saw how happy it made you, that's when I decided to let Jacob stay. If I didn't want him here, I would've said no right from the start and stuck to it. But I didn't. I let him stay.'

'Well, can you explain where he's disappeared to then?'

'No, I can't. It doesn't make the least bit of sense, and I can't explain what's happened because I simply don't know. Maybe you went sleepwalking and opened the door – maybe that's what happened.'

'Don't be ridiculous, Mark. I don't sleepwalk.'

'Well, I don't know how else it could have happened. All I know is, it wasn't me. For some reason you keep thinking I want to hurt you, but I don't. Why do you think that?'

'It's because everyone wants to hurt me.'

I no longer knew what Sarah was talking about. She continued squawking and squealing and saying ridiculous things. In my calmest voice, I tried to reason with her, but she was off-limits. For all I knew, she could have let Jacob go on purpose just to start another argument with me. It could all have been premeditated. Or maybe she wasn't the only one who was paranoid.

For the rest of the day things returned to the way they'd been before Jacob's arrival. The atmosphere had soured and I had no idea how to turn things around.

# visitors and the red dressing gown

Most of December had drifted by. Despite this, Christmas seemed impossibly remote and distant. I was numb to the festive spirit. Any Christmas cheer that I was exposed to, which mainly came through the medium of TV, was ignored point blank. For Sarah and me, Christmas was a non-event this year. This was mainly due to Sarah's low mood, but another big factor was the monetary problems we were having. Neither of us had a job anymore. There was no money whatsoever coming in, and whatever savings we'd had were being swallowed up fast by our crippling mortgage and the never-ending stream of bills that landed through the letterbox each day. Most of the envelopes stayed unopened, especially the ones with bold red writing on them – the final reminders. Despite the pressure we were under, I thought we had enough money saved to see us through to January, maybe even February at a push, but that would mean cancelling Christmas altogether – no gifts, no turkey, not even cards. Then after the holidays I would start a proper search for a job, and Sarah would be better, and everything would be back to normal. That was the plan.

That Saturday afternoon I lay inert on the couch. My long, greasy hair now covered my ears and poked at my eyes. The heavy stubble I'd allowed to grow had turned into a full beard. The hair was thick and grizzled. I was almost unrecognisable to myself. I wasn't expecting anyone to call and wasn't prepared when I heard a knock on the front door. I had to think quickly. Did I want to answer it and run the risk of talking to someone when I really didn't wish to? Or could this visit lead to something worthwhile?

In my socks, I glided silently to the front door. Pressing my palms against it, I peeked closely through the peephole. It was William and Penny, bearing armfuls of gifts. Part of me wanted to leave the door unanswered, to let them walk away. But they'd obviously gone to a lot of trouble, and I knew that if I did ignore them guilt would catch up with me later in the day, making me feel worse than I already did. So hesitantly I opened the door. William and Penny greeted me with joyous smiles once they were over the shock of my changed appearance. They stepped inside without waiting to be asked and made their own way into the living room. They both looked confused to see it devoid of decorations.

'Where's your Christmas tree?' Penny asked.

'We're not having one this year.'

'You're not? Why not?'

'With all that's happened recently, we're not really in the mood for Christmas.'

'That's a shame,' she said, and looked sidelong at William.

There was an awkward silence. I was happy when he spoke up.

'What are you doing just now?' he asked.

'Not much. I've not been doing much for a long time.'

'What do you mean?'

'It's a long story.'

'Well, why don't you tell me about it over a pint? D'you fancy going for one right now?'

'I'm not sure.'

'Come on. We can get a pint, maybe even two, and the girls can have a chat and a catch up.'

'Well, maybe that would be good. It might help Sarah if she speaks to you, Penny. She's not really been speaking to me.'

'So it's settled then,' William said, excitedly. 'I'm gagging on a pint,' he added.

'Okay then. Let's do it.'

'Don't be out for long though. An hour … hour and a half at the most,' Penny warned us.

'Sure thing. We won't be long at all,' William said, and kissed her on the cheek.

'So where is Sarah?' Penny asked.

'I'm guessing she's still in bed. She hardly moves from it nowadays. It'll be good for her to see you,' I said.

'Let's hope so,' Penny replied.

Before we left, I slipped on a pair of shoes and grabbed my jacket and scarf. Then William and I made our way out into the cold. As I hadn't left the house for the best part of a week, the chill hit me harder than it had all winter.

We made our way up to the main street, exchanging small talk about the weather. William then spoke about work before changing the subject to his hatred of Christmas shopping and how he couldn't stand helping Penny with it, although he was forced to. He was a talking machine. He was too hyper and sometimes hard to take, but on this occasion I was happy for him to tell me anything, any amount of ambiguous bullshit he could muster up, just so long as I didn't have to contribute to the conversation too much.

There were a number of pubs and bars to choose from, but they were all the same, all a bit dodgy. The one we agreed to visit was called the Oak Inn. It was a place that I didn't dare ever visit on my own or at night, due to violence and fuckwits and certain stories that I'd heard. But I was sure we'd be safe enough on a Saturday afternoon, if we kept our heads down.

Inside, we were met by the stale smell of beer and dust. It was dull and grotty. The carpet was studded with hardened chewing gum. Only the fruit machine's flashing neon lights brightened the interior slightly.

There was a mix of different people inside, some young, some old, some who looked at home there and others awkward and wary, just like us. There was a group of young men in their late teens or early twenties, sitting at a round table, continuously downing shots of an unknown alcoholic substance. They all wore matching tracksuits and looked like part of a football team or some other kind of sports club. They were loud and brash, best avoided. And then there were the old ones, the alcoholic geriatrics, who sat directly at the bar, as close to the booze as possible. Some were missing teeth, and the others sporting full sets probably wore false ones. Most had fine, thinning hair, if any. Their skin was slightly jaundiced, but worst of all they stank. They had that peculiar odour, the one that seems to follow old people around, the kind that they're apparently oblivious to.

I let William buy the first round while I found a table. I got one that was hidden away in the most secluded part of the pub, right in the corner. I sat down and watched him order our drinks while trying to dodge being sucked into conversation with the old geezers. He came back with two pints in his hands, sat down and sighed out loud.

'Fucking hell – what an absolute bunch of weirdos in here!'

'I know. I'm sorry about that, but at least it's kind of warm.'

'Yeah, too right, man. I was freezing my nuts off out there.'

'Me too. Even with layers on, the chill still gets through to your bones.'

'You can say that again,' he said, and then veered straight off on another topic. 'When I was up at the bar, some old guy started talking to me as if I knew him.'

He pointed to the man in question. He was short, bald and hunchbacked, wearing a leather jacket that looked to be at least fifty years old. The jacket was probably once black but had weathered the way old leather does.

'He asked me if I'd heard of some guy. I can't remember what name he said, but when I told him that I didn't live out this way, he began giving me the third degree, asking me all these weird questions. I just ignored him. Fucking alky.'

'Yeah, they're all a bit special in here.'

'So, Mark, what's been happening? I've not seen you since ... since ... you know.'

He didn't want to say it, but he meant James's funeral.

'I know. It's been bad. It's been totally shit.'

I took a long gulp from my pint, bracing myself for the heart-to-heart that I could feel was forthcoming.

'You're not doing well then,' said William. It was a statement, not a question.

'No. I'm not sure if you've heard, but I lost my job.'

'Nah, I didn't know that. What happened?'

'It's a long fucked-up story. I can't really be bothered going through it all again, but in the end I was given an ultimatum and I decided to walk.'

'That's fair enough, I suppose.'

'Not if you knew what I did, it isn't. But apart from that, I've been doing okay.'

'Are you looking for another job just now?'

'I've looked a little, but nothing's come up. I'm going

to wait until after Christmas and then start looking properly.'

'You still want to teach though?'

'I don't know. I don't really care what I do. Really, I'd sit on a till scanning shit all day if it meant making some money.'

'Are you struggling then – financially, I mean?'

'Yeah, but we'll manage somehow. I do need to tell you though, and I'm quite embarrassed about it, but we won't be buying you guys presents this year. In fact, we're not buying presents for anyone. We simply can't afford it.'

'Don't worry about it, man. We're all too old for presents nowadays anyway. There are more important things going on.'

'Damn right.'

'I've got an idea,' William said, enthusiastically.

'What's that then?'

'How about I lend you some money, just a little to see you through?'

'I don't think so.'

'Come on, man. It'll be between us. The girls don't need to know about it.'

'I'm not sure.'

'I'm not talking about thousands of pounds here, maybe just a couple of hundred to tide you over.'

'I'm not sure ...'

Although I said that, really, I wanted to bite his hand off at the offer.

'Please, I'd like to help you out. You're one of the good guys. What do you say?'

'If I do say yes, I promise I'll pay you back with my next pay packet, whenever that may be.'

'Sure. If that's what you want to do, it's fine by me.'

'Only a couple of hundred though.'

'Yeah, if that's all you need.'

'Okay then. I'll take you up on your offer,' I said, shaking his hand. 'I really appreciate it, man. I really fucking appreciate it.'

'It's not a problem. On our way back we can go via a cash machine and I'll get you the moolah.'

'Cheers.'

'And I reckon you should use some of it to buy Sarah a present. You don't need to bother with anyone else, just her.'

'I might do that. A present could help things, I guess.'

'So to change the subject, how is she?'

'Terrible,' I said, bluntly. 'Since losing James, we seem to be going through endless sequences of horrible events, a never-ending river of shit.'

'That's rough, man.'

'I know. I've had the doctor out, I've tried being nice to her, I've tried all sorts of things, but she doesn't want to know. She's stuck in a bubble right now and she doesn't want to burst it to get free.'

'It must have been hard for her though.'

'I know that, but somehow she needs to try and move

on. Doing what she's doing right now isn't helping anyone.'

'Is there anything that Penny and I could do?'

'I don't think so. If her own husband can't even help her then I don't know how you guys could. I think she needs to fight her own way through this. Thanks for the offer though.'

'No worries.'

'To be honest, I'm quite glad to get out of the house. Since my newfound unemployment, I've been wallowing on the couch most days, vegetating. It's good to be out again, and this beer tastes good too.'

'Good stuff. Cheers to that.'

By the end of the conversation we'd finished our drinks. When I tried to get up and buy another round, William wouldn't allow it. We went back and forth, having a jovial argument about who should pay; eventually I gave up, and he went back to the bar.

He returned with another two pints and our conversation moved from the serious to the absurd. We had the usual banter that you'd expect to hear in a pub. We spoke about stuff that didn't matter, and it felt good. I felt good. I was relaxed and worry-free. William, on the other hand, was keeping a close eye on the time. He'd stare up at the antique-looking clock that hung on the wall, or he'd look at his watch, or he'd check the time on his mobile phone. He seemed edgy. I quizzed him on his actions and he wasn't shy of telling me how under the thumb he was with

Penny. We both agreed to down our pints quickly, giving us enough time to squeeze in another before we had to leave. I told him straight off that I'd pay for the last ones, and he tentatively accepted.

At the bar, I managed to avoid making eye contact with anyone, apart from the barman that is, and made it back to my seat safely without having to talk to any of the old drunkards. Like the last ones, these pints slipped down the hatch smoothly and quickly, and we were slightly tipsy as we left the pub.

We were surprised by the sight that met us. Snow had fallen. It couldn't have been coming down for long as only a thin layer had settled on the paths and roads. Simultaneously, we both stood still and put our right hands into the air. We held them steady, letting the soft, fluffy flakes of pure white snow land in our palms. And then we watched the flakes dissolve, turning to water on our warm-blooded skin.

We crossed the road at the traffic lights and stopped at the cash machine. William did what he needed to do and handed me the two hundred pounds that we'd agreed on, all in twenty-pound notes. I took the money from him, putting it safely into my wallet, then my wallet into the pocket of my jeans, and then I shook his hand again. As we walked back to the flat, he took out his mobile phone and answered an incoming call.

'Hi, Penny. We're just on our way back now.'

He spoke straight away, trying to pre-empt her moaning.

I didn't take any notice of what he was saying until I heard his exclamation.

'You're kidding, right? She's actually locked you in there? Christ! Okay, don't panic – we'll be back in a minute or so. We'll be as quick as we can.'

He lowered the phone from his ear, and shook his head at me. I asked him what had happened, and he told me. Sarah had locked Penny in the bathroom.

We ran back to the flat. Despite the cold air and the fresh falling snow, we were both sweating as we entered. There was a chair propped against the handle of the bathroom door, stopping Penny from turning it and getting out. I took the chair away and opened the door. She came out shaking and understandably upset. Tears filled her eyes. I don't think she was upset because she had been locked in the bathroom, more because her own sister could do something like that to her. She wrapped her arms around William and cried into his snow-covered jacket.

'What happened, Penny?' I asked.

'I don't know,' she sobbed. 'For a while I was talking to her in the bedroom and everything seemed fine, and then I had to go to the toilet and that's when I heard her moving around. I heard something being put up against the door, and when I was finished I couldn't get out. I shouted and shouted for Sarah but she didn't come. It's lucky I took my bag and my phone with me or I'd still be stuck in there.'

'Was she upset with you about anything?'

'Not that I know of. We were just chatting, although it was me doing most of the talking, but she didn't seem cross about anything. She didn't even get out of bed.'

'For fuck's sake,' I said. 'I'm getting really sick of all this bullshit!'

'Go easy, man,' William said. 'It'll get better soon.'

'I don't think so,' I told him.

'It will,' he said, positively.

*It won't,* I thought to myself. As William consoled Penny, I made my way to the squalid bedroom in search of Sarah, but all I found was the grubby duvet slung across the empty bed. Sarah wasn't there. I checked the rest of the flat, but the rooms were empty. I joined William and Penny again in the hallway outside the bathroom door.

'She's not here!' I said, worriedly.

'What do you mean, she's not here?' asked Penny.

'I mean she's not fucking here!'

'Easy, Mark. Just calm down a second,' said William.

'I swear to God, I can't handle this anymore. What am I going to do with her?'

There were tears rolling down my face now as well as Penny's. William was the only person holding it together, not crying.

'Come on, let's sit down, see if we can get our heads around this,' he said.

William put an arm around each of our shoulders and steered us into the living room. Instead of discussing where Sarah could be, though, we sat in silence. William did occasionally try to brighten the mood by making some of his inane remarks but it was to no avail. Soon enough he stopped trying and made drinks for us instead. Penny had a cup of tea, but seeing that we were already half-cut, he and I had something stronger. There seemed no point in sobering up. We had vodka. As we drank, we all stayed quiet.

'What if she's run away somewhere?' Penny blurted out, rupturing the silence.

'She's not run away,' William replied.

'But what if she has? We should call the police.'

'Don't be stupid, Penny. The police aren't going to give a crap. She's only been gone an hour or so. She'll be back soon.'

'Well, we should at least be out there searching for her. I mean, look at the snow now, just look how heavy it's coming down,' she said, pointing towards the window. 'Sarah could freeze to death out there.'

'Don't say things like that! Don't ever say things like that!' I said angrily, pointing my finger straight in Penny's face, which upset her even more.

I got to my feet and walked over to the window. Through the thick double-glazed glass, I watched the snow fall. The sky was full of it and the streets were covered. The scene outside didn't look real. It was as if I were staring into a giant snow globe after someone had shaken it. Maybe the world was God's little snow globe, I thought.

As I stared through the gusts of white powder that filled the air, I saw something bright moving against the snow. It was a lady in red, and she was walking towards the building. There was no need for me to see her face – I knew it was Sarah. It was her walk. It was her red dressing gown, the one I'd bought for her last Christmas. I ran out of the living room. William and Penny asked where I was going, but there was no time to answer – I had to get to her.

I made it down the stairwell and to the entrance of the building just as Sarah came in from the blizzard. She was shaking as if in the throes of an epileptic fit. All she was wearing was the dressing gown, which was now covered in a layer of snow, along with whatever underwear she had on beneath. Her bare feet were red raw. I didn't know what to expect from her, but she walked straight by me as if I wasn't even there, making her way up the winding stairs. I walked behind her. When we reached our floor, William and Penny were waiting for us by the front door. As soon as Penny caught sight of her sister she ran straight to her, throwing her arms around Sarah's shivering body. Sarah stood there numb, arms resting by her sides, still shaking and breathing heavily.

'I'm so glad you're safe,' said Penny. 'Where have you been? We've all been worried sick,' she added, slackening her grip.

'I've been out,' Sarah replied, as if to do so in her dressing gown in a snowstorm was perfectly normal.

'I'm not bothered that you locked me in there.' Penny pointed to the bathroom. 'But you can't run off in the snow like that.'

'I didn't run off. I've just been out.'

'You're not well, Sarah. You understand that, don't you? There's something not right with you!'

I could tell by Sarah's expression that Penny had hit a nerve.

'I didn't want you here in the first place. I don't want any of you here! Why can't you people just leave me alone?'

'We're your family. We're only trying to help.'

'You can help me by pissing off. I want you all to leave right now! Get the hell out of my home!'

'What?' Penny asked in disbelief.

She'd never seen this side of her older, supposedly wiser sister before.

'I mean it. I want everyone to leave – now!'

'Sarah, just calm down and think for a second,' said William.

'No! This is my home, and I want you all to go. So go!'

'Well, I'm not going anywhere,' I said. 'This is as much my home as it is yours, so I'm staying.'

'Whatever you say. I'm going to bed. But I want *you* and *you* to go, now!' she said, pointing to William and Penny and then the open door.

She walked away from us without a care in the world – no guilt, no worries, and no weight on her shoulders.

William and Penny were stunned. They couldn't believe that Sarah would talk to them like that. They hadn't yet been exposed to her drastic character change. Penny wanted to go back into the bedroom and reason with her, but I didn't allow it. I couldn't. On Sarah's behalf, I apologised for her actions and attitude, and made a promise that I'd turn things around and we'd see them on Christmas Day.

# the 23rd of december

I looked out of the window. The snow hadn't stopped for days. Outside, it was a winter paradise. The once grey streets were now beautifully fresh and bright, the perfect setting for Christmas. A regular Christmas that is, not this Christmas, not ours.

In an attempt to make the flat more festive, I strategically positioned the Christmas cards we'd received throughout the living room. I put them in places that would catch Sarah's eye, in the hope of cheering her up, reminding her what time of year it was. I paid the box room a visit, where I unearthed some tinsel from a black bin bag in which we kept all the decorations. I wrapped strands of gold, silver and red tinsel around various pictures on the walls. If it didn't help anything, at least it made the place a little more colourful. That was my plan of action – minor decorations and a gift. Finding the gift was my next move. With my heaviest winter clothes on, I was ready to brave the arctic conditions outside. Before I left, I made a cup of tea for Sarah, her special tea: milk, with her regular dosage of two antidepressant capsule powders mixed in. My tactic hadn't worked thus far, but I felt I had to persist. What else did I have to work with?

I wore my walking boots when I went out, ploughing through the snow heaped on the pavements. Most of the streets were deserted. The only visible bodies were those of three people shovelling their driveways. I wanted to ask them why they were doing it now while the snow was still falling. Surely it would make more sense to wait until it had stopped. But asking meant talking, and I didn't want to talk.

I turned the corner to catch the bus into Princes Street, and that's when I found everyone. There was a gigantic queue of people waiting at the bus stop. I guessed they were all last-minute shoppers like me, but at least I had good reasons for my lateness. I joined the queue and waited patiently. With the snow-covered roads, there weren't many vehicles out and those that were travelled at a snail's pace. I didn't mind waiting. I've always been fairly patient. But the people standing beside me had a different view of things – they moaned that they'd been waiting for an hour without any sign of a bus. I wanted to shake them. I wanted to prise their eyes open, force them to look at the thick covering of snow on the ground. I wanted to pick up fistfuls of it and shove it in their mouths. While listening to their bullshit, I was the first to notice a double-decker bus coming into view, driving slowly in our direction. It felt like a victory over the fools standing next to me, as I'd only been waiting for five minutes.

As the bus drew closer, I could see that most of the seats were occupied and was doubtful we would all get on. I myself was at the very back of the queue.

The bus stopped; the doors opened. People filtered in, the queue at the bus stop gradually diminishing. Surprisingly, the driver managed to squeeze everyone on board, even me. Downstairs, people were standing, squashed up too close together for my liking. Out of curiosity more than anything else, I went upstairs. I'd assumed that other people would have tried their luck already and all the seats would be taken, but they weren't. There was still one free. It was right at the front, looking straight out of the window. It felt like my lucky day. I sat down and took my woollen gloves off. Using one of them, I wiped away the condensation that had formed on the inside of the glass, allowing me to see where we were going. Then I sat back in the seat, closed my eyes, and fell into a doze.

I hadn't dreamed about James for quite some time, but as I began to drift off I found myself back in the white world. Sarah was there, holding James in her arms, but that was as far as the dream went. It was abruptly interrupted by the clamour of the other passengers on board.

The noise was loud but distorted. There were a lot of voices, saying nothing I could understand. With so many people talking at once, the words melted together into a dull roar. During the slow drive, I managed to switch off, keeping my mind a blank. That was until the sound of a single screeching voice cut through the others. I found myself instantly on the alert. I listened closely, waiting, wanting to hear it again, and then it came: a cackle of laughter and a loud, intrusive voice, one that was unmistakable. Straight away panic set in, sweat began rolling down my back and the palpitations started.

At first I didn't want to turn around, but I had to be certain. Surely I couldn't be this unlucky. I slid down in my seat, turned my head, and peered down the aisle over rows of unrecognisable faces. My actions must have looked strange. From where I was sitting, I could see only those in the aisle seats. None of them looked familiar. As I looked on, though, I heard that voice again and it triggered something inside me.

I sprang up from my seat and stared straight down the gangway. I had a view of everyone on the top deck, and now I could see him clearly – Kyle McGuire. He was sitting at the very back of the bus, tucked away in the right-hand corner, surrounded by his entourage of cronies. He raised his head, looked straight at me. The cocky smile he was sporting instantly transformed into a grimace. The friends sitting around him carried on joking, messing around, oblivious to our face-off. It was like we were the only two people on the overfilled bus. We stared at each other long and hard.

In my head, I ran through an alternative scene, one that I desperately wanted to act out. I'd run up the aisle, grab Kyle by his collar, drag him over the seats, and then pin him down on the floor and repeatedly punch him in the face until he bled. Once he'd had enough of that, I would throw him down the stairs head first. And then, if there was still the slightest trace of a smile or a smirk on his battered face, I would hit the emergency stop button and throw him out of the bus, straight into oncoming traffic.

There was still a long way to go until we reached the city centre. However, I couldn't stay on the bus listening to his mindless drivel any longer or stand the sight of his leering face. If I stayed I definitely would do him damage. Just the thought of it made me smile straight at him. Kyle looked puzzled. I rang the bell, walked down the stairs and got off at the next stop. Part of me wished that I'd done something to make him realise what a shit-bag he really was.

After a few seconds, I heard the sound of tapping. I raised my eyes towards the top deck of the bus. Kyle was staring down at me from the nearside window. As the vehicle started pulling away, he stuck his middle finger up at me. I immediately regretted not doing anything to him. Too late. I ran unsteadily through the snow until I reached the back-end of the bus and gave it a volley of kicks, which only caused harm to my own freezing toes. He'd won again, the little shit.

Trudging through the canvas of thick snow that lay underfoot, it was hard not to think about Kyle; somehow, though, I had to put it to the back of my mind. Worrying about one spotty teenager wasn't my priority. He was an attention-seeking little prick and nothing more. I couldn't let the thought of him wind me up. Sarah was the only important thing left in my life now. Today was all about her. It took me a good hour to make it to Princes Street. By this point in the afternoon, the winter sun was already setting.

Town was a mass of people. There were thousands upon thousands of them, marching in and out of shops like armies of ants, the only difference being that they weren't working together. They were all out for themselves. People seemed oblivious to the existence of others. I watched endless numbers of them walk unapologetically into one another. To escape the crowds on the pavement, I dived into the first large department store I came to.

Once out of the revolving door, I was hit by a wall of noise, warmth, and rushing people. It was chaotic. Christmas shopping was never my forte. In the past, Sarah had actually enjoyed it. Why would anyone enjoy it? I found it overwhelming, almost unbearable. Deep breaths were taken as I tried to stay on top of my frustration and claustrophobia. I didn't last long in that first store. I didn't even look at anything. I entered, drifted around in a cold, panicky sweat, and then escaped through the revolving door as soon as I could. Being back out in the crisp, biting, fresh air felt good, but I was no further forward in my quest for Sarah's gift, my chance of redemption.

Most of the snow that lay in the city-centre streets had been tracked through with grit, which meant it was now a mixture of white and dirty brown. To the right of me was Edinburgh Castle. It was a beautiful sight, one that in better days had always aroused a frisson of pride in me.

Now, seeing the castle lit up with bright blue lights, that feeling slowly returned. The deeper I walked into town towards the east end, the more joyous things became. Amusements were brought in specifically for the festive months. The sky was illuminated with a rainbow of neon lights, most of which were coming from the spectacularly large Ferris wheel positioned next to its antithesis, the Scott Monument, a dull, creepy, Gothic monument, but a historic one. The sight of the big wheel and the dazzling lights made me want to see more, so I temporarily abandoned my shopping mission, crossed the road, and walked into the gardens.

The German market was the first thing I came to. Row upon row of wooden shacks filled the space, each selling something different. They sold all sorts – knitted hats, handmade wooden toys, jams, sausages – but the busiest one by far was the stall selling mulled wine.

It proved to be difficult manoeuvring my way through the crowds, but surprisingly the claustrophobia that I'd experienced in the store only a short time earlier didn't return. From where I stood in the gardens, I was able to look down and view the ice rink. Skaters were falling over while onlookers laughed at them, everyone enjoying the fun. The atmosphere that I found myself immersed in was such a positive one that it was beginning to rub off on me. It was hard to resist. It was hard not to be seduced by the howls of laughter, the glee reflected from the smiling faces all around. However, seeing all those loved-up couples and happy families made me wish I wasn't there alone. That was the only drawback for me, the only negative side to being here. I walked through the gardens, drinking in the ambiance, and then I walked back out on to the street again, into the hustle and bustle, ready to resume the task in hand.

I took a deep breath before crossing the road. I was back on the side with all the crowds hell-bent on shopping. Another department store was my destination. It was the biggest, the oldest, and the most traditional store in the city. Things appeared to be calmer in this one. I was glad of that. However, I was still unsure of what to get Sarah, and walked around like a lost puppy. I looked at various things – clothes, bags, perfumes, jewellery – but they didn't seem appropriate. While browsing, I left myself open to the attentions of teenaged sales assistants, who seemed to be fully aware of my vulnerable disposition and were unsympathetically trying to cash in on it. They were hunting me down in packs, hounding me, but somehow I managed to escape without being bitten.

I explored each floor of the large building in detail, looking for something worthwhile. Time was ticking by and so far nothing had grabbed my attention. I wanted something personal, not just another possession. It didn't have to be expensive, lavish or fancy; it didn't have to sparkle. It just had to be right. Then unexpectedly something caught my eye. It was simple, silly, sentimental. It was a white photo frame with the words 'I will always love you' inscribed on it in red writing. As soon as I saw it, I knew exactly whose picture would fill that empty frame. Without looking at anything else, I took it to the till, paid for it, and left the store. My job was done.

Before getting the bus home, I went to a card shop. It was inundated with people. I had to fight my way through the other customers to collect the things that I needed: a roll of wrapping paper, a packet of tags, some Sellotape. I made my way to the till in order to pay for them. The queue stretched all the way to the rear wall of the shop before doubling round. I'd had enough. I wasn't going to wait again. With a rush of blood to the head, I turned my back on everyone and put the items I wanted to buy into my jacket, which was big and padded enough for me to be able to conceal the things without it looking obvious. All the shop assistants were busily attending to paying customers, so I grabbed my opportunity and quickly strode out of the shop. In that second, I crossed the line from would-be customer to petty thief. But I have to admit that I found it exhilarating. Looking over my shoulder, I waited for someone to come after me and give chase. It didn't happen. I crossed the road again, making my way to the bus stop. This wait was much longer. Maybe I'd used up all my luck for the day, but unlike the other people waiting, I wasn't angry. I was happy to bide my time.

When the bus came, I got on and was overcome with déjà vu. Downstairs was packed. People were standing, squashed up tight, as on the journey in. I made my way upstairs in the hope of finding a seat. As I trudged up each step, my stomach churned. There was a bad feeling in it. For some reason, I thought I'd see Kyle's face again, and that he'd be sitting in exactly the same seat as he had been earlier. And if he was there, how would I control myself? I reached the top. My eyes scanned everyone, scrutinising their faces, and I received a few inquisitive stares in return, but thankfully there was no sign of Kyle. There was no sign of a free seat either so I had no choice but to return downstairs and take my place amongst the huddle of equally worn-out passengers.

I rode the bus home, balancing on my aching feet, clutching the gift that was going to save Sarah and me in my hand. With traffic moving slowly and cautiously, it took a fair amount of time to get home. I stood clinging to one of the metal poles. My eyes kept shutting, but snapped open whenever the bus hit a pothole or when a passenger rang the bell to get off. After this had happened a few times, I shook my head vigorously to wake myself up. I opened the window next to me, allowing a gust of icy air to enter and bite at my tired eyes. This annoyed a few of my fellow passengers, and they gave me scowling looks. I left the window open. It helped me, and being able to help yourself now and again is no crime.

Finally we were back in Corstorphine. I made my way to the front of the bus. Once I moved away, a man immediately got up from his seat and slammed the window shut. He looked at me, and then muttered something to the passenger sitting beside him. I smiled to myself and got off. Christmas can push people both ways, good and bad, beautiful and ugly.

After all the trekking that I'd done in the snow, my so-called water-resistant boots were sodden, my toes wet and stinging. On the walk back to the flat, I saw two out of the three people who'd been clearing their driveways earlier still going at it. That was hour upon hour ago. They couldn't have had anything better to do with their lives than stand outside in an endless limbo of snow. Frozen and solemn-faced, they looked more as if they were digging graves. I bounced past them with jaunty, springing steps, eager to be home again. At our building, I entered the stairwell. It was eerily quiet. Usually you'd hear some sort of noise from the neighbours, their kids, pets, music, something, but right now there wasn't a whisper. All I could hear were my own footsteps and the way my breath caught in my chest as I pounded up the staircase. I got to our floor, put my key in the front door and opened it.

The flat too was silent, the bedroom door still closed. It didn't seem as if Sarah had moved all day. Nothing looked out of place; nothing seemed to have been touched since I'd left. I went into the living room, closed the door and then took out the photo frame that I'd bought, along with the wrapping materials I'd stolen.

I got the photo, the one on which I'd placed all my

hopes. It was the one from our honeymoon, the one that I'd kept in my desk when I'd worked at the school. I slid it into the frame and it fitted perfectly. That felt like a good sign. Something that was meant to be. A rush of energy, adrenaline, and happiness surged wildly through me. I was sure now that my plan would work. It would make Sarah realise that things could be good again between us, that she still loved me. I couldn't wait to turn her mood around so we could love each other again as we used to. With unsteady hands, I cut the wrapping paper, folded it around the frame, wrote out a tag, and that was it. I was done. All I had to do was wait for the 25th to arrive and pray that my plan would be successful.

# the hell days of christmas

Sarah's present was wrapped and ready to go. I felt good even if my walking and shopping had drained me. I spent the rest of the day sprawled on the couch, recuperating while I watched TV. The adrenaline had worn off by now. I felt as if all the energy had been drained from me. The day seemed normal enough: Sarah in the bedroom, me in the living room. That was our pattern these days. It wasn't until I went to the bathroom that I found out something was wrong. Oh, so devastatingly wrong. I didn't close or lock the door, in case Sarah tried to repeat the mean trick she'd played on Penny. I lifted up the toilet seat and began urinating. I zoned out, staring at the tiled wall directly ahead of me. I noticed the grout sealing the tiles. I stared at it deeply, observing the once liquid mixture that had now hardened and was serving a purpose. I was unsure why I was suddenly so absorbed by something I looked at every day. Maybe my mind was already at work, trying to protect me.

I buttoned up my jeans and tightened my belt. Without looking in the sink, I turned the hot tap on and put my hands underneath the running water. When I looked down at my hands and the sink beneath them, I saw blood. I checked my hands thoroughly, expecting to see some sort of wound or cut, but they were clean and unscratched. Moving my hands out of view, I saw the very definition of horror: two bloodied razor blades being rinsed clean by the water splashing down on top of them. They were my blades, my shaving blades, from the days when I actually used to care about my appearance. I felt sick. I knew instantly what had happened. With that realisation my legs gave way and I had to hold on to the sink to stop myself from collapsing. As I struggled to stay afoot, my eyes moved down to the white-tiled floor. More blood. On trembling legs, I hurried to the bedroom. Passing through the hallway, I noticed further pools of red staining the floor. How I'd missed them when I'd initially gone to the toilet was bewildering, but somehow I had, and somehow I managed to make it to the bedroom without falling flat on my face.

On the surface there was nothing out of the ordinary in the scene before me. Sarah lay under the covers with her head tilted to the right, resting on the pillow. It was a sight I'd observed many times over the last two months, one that was more than familiar to me. As I approached her, I looked for traces of blood on the white duvet. There was nothing visible. The closer I got, the more unsettled I felt. I knew what she'd done; I just hoped I'd found her in time and there was still a chance to save her life.

Her face was pale and getting paler. As I stood over her, I swear I could see the last traces of life draining from her, right before my eyes. I stroked her cheek. The skin felt cold and tight. With a sharp movement I pulled back the duvet and confirmed what I already knew. Sarah was naked, her stick-thin body covered in dark blood, blood that was mainly dry but still a little sticky. Her wrists were pressed down into the mattress. I noticed that her fingers were stuck together with clotted blood. Her wedding and engagement rings were invisible beneath it. With a churning sensation in my stomach, I turned her wrists over, revealing a ghastly sight. She'd done it properly, not the way you see in films. She'd slit them down the way, vertically. That was the correct way, not across, not horizontally. The long wounds were still seeping blood, but the damage had been done. Sarah was dead.

Next to her in the bed lay a box of pills. I read the label with a sick feeling coming over me. These were the antidepressants I'd been sneakily feeding her for the past few weeks. Somehow she'd found them. Or maybe she'd known all along what I'd been up to. The sight of those pills crushed me. I was drowning in guilt. The blisters within the box were all popped open, which meant she'd gobbled close to thirty capsules. Those pills were supposed to help her live again; instead they'd helped her die.

It struck me then that she'd used two ways of killing herself, and strangely I found some comfort in that. It meant that her mind was clear, her choice decisive. If slitting her wrists didn't do it then the pills would, or vice versa. It was something that she'd really had to do, something she'd wanted. By this point tears were streaming from my eyes, and I heard the harsh, disjointed sounds of my own sobbing. The sight was so horrible, so surreal. It was hard to comprehend that the lifeless body in the bed was that of my first girlfriend, later my wife, and now she was gone, completely gone. Beside the box of pills was an empty white wine bottle. She must have washed down the pills with that. The bed sheet was sodden. Splashes of wine, blood, and urine dampened it. Despite this, I sat down on my side of the bed next to her.

In my head, I was screaming with pain but couldn't vocalise the sounds. Shock had taken hold of me. I wept, but I wasn't hysterical. The more I thought about all the things we'd been through over the last two months, the more inevitable her suicide seemed. I should have seen it coming a mile off. If only I'd opened my eyes and my mind a little more, maybe I could have saved her. The fear of her doing something drastic had always lurked unacknowledged in my thoughts, but I'd believed she'd escape her depression, given space and time. I looked at her sadly diminished form once more and the terrible state it was in. Then I wondered about a note. Surely she'd written one, telling me and her family how much she loved us and that it wasn't our fault. Surely she'd done that. Surely such a note was mandatory for a suicide. Removing the duvet fully from the bed, I threw it on the floor.

There was a piece of paper trapped under her bare thigh. It took both my arms to lift her stiff leg, and then I took the folded, blood-spotted note out from under it.

Before I looked at it, I covered Sarah's wounded body again with the duvet and sat down beside her. My hands were shaking badly as I unfolded the paper, expecting to find words. There were none. This was better than words.

To my amazement, on the sheet of paper was a drawing. It was identical to the one that James had done in my dream. It was the same drawing that I'd spent a whole night trying unsuccessfully to replicate. I had no idea how Sarah had done it. All my efforts were destroyed, burned, without her ever seeing them. It didn't make sense – unless she'd been having dreams similar to mine, similar realistic dreams. Or maybe we'd had the same dreams at the same times. For me the drawing was better than any note, better than any explanation. Seeing the three of us depicted like that, together and happy, was a beautiful thing. Being a family was all that Sarah and I had ever wanted, and losing James had meant the end of it all. This picture put us back together.

I didn't know what to do. I didn't call an ambulance or the police; I didn't call Sarah's parents or her sister. I didn't call my parents. I didn't do anything. Instead, I held on to the drawing while I slid under the duvet, and stared at the ceiling. My brain felt scrambled. I thought about the photo frame that I'd bought for Sarah, and how if Christmas had come just two days earlier that gift might have saved her. Then again, maybe nothing would have changed, but now I'd never know.

For an unknown number of days I didn't move. I lay under the duvet with Sarah's withering body. Occasionally I would speak to her, asking questions in the receding hope of receiving a reply. I'd recall some of the good times we'd had together, and smile. I'm not sure how many days went by, and although I was in bed, I didn't fall asleep once.

I could tell when morning arrived by the sunrise that glowed through the window, and could tell when night fell when the room sank into darkness. But even then my eyes remained open and I stayed awake. Sometimes I'd look out of the window. I'd follow snowflakes as they fell from the sky, or birds as they flew on by. After a while, sleep deprivation kicked in and I began to hallucinate. Strange visions were appearing before me. The most terrifying ones were those featuring Sarah. When I looked at her face her eyes would be open, staring back at me, and her mouth would be moving, spilling out words. I managed to cling on to reality enough to tell myself that none of it was real. I knew that my tired, overwrought mind was playing awful tricks on me.

One day the phone rang constantly, but I didn't answer. Later, someone knocked on the door and I heard the voices of William and Penny resonate through the letterbox, but I didn't respond to them. Eventually they left. With all the activity, it must have been Christmas Day.

As the days passed I continued not to eat. My belly howled with hunger, begged for food, but I resisted its pleadings. My sandpaper-dry mouth was crying out for water, but I stayed in bed. I was losing control of myself and in any case had nothing left to live for. The world had turned into a place that I couldn't face, not alone, not without Sarah. My own time had arrived. I had to follow the same route as she had. Make my escape from the world.

I thought about how I was going to do it. Would I copy her method of pills, wine and razor blades, or would I try something different? I wanted it to be instant and painless. The thought of cutting my wrists, allowing blood to drain from me slowly, wasn't appealing. Likewise pills. Overdosing on drugs would mean internal and mind-altering side effects, which I wasn't keen on experiencing. I'd had enough of them already.

Finally I got out of the bed, weak with starvation, and went to the wardrobe. I knew now how I was going to do it. I got changed into a shirt and tie, put on a black suit and a pair of polished black shoes. It was pretty much the same outfit that I'd worn to James's funeral. Once changed, I went to the bathroom, combed my hair and brushed my teeth. My face was gaunt and pale. I saw in the mirror, under the thick covering of facial hair, only a poor imitation of the man I used to be.

The razor blades that Sarah had used to slice open her veins still lay in the sink. I picked one up and began using it to remove the hair from my face. I didn't use any water or shaving foam. I managed to remove most of my beard without cutting up my face too much. There seemed something fitting about using the same blade as Sarah had. Once I'd finished, I looked slightly better, a little more like my old self. I lifted the second razor blade out of the sink. I dried them both with a towel and put them in my trouser pocket. I dampened the same towel with warm water and wiped up the blood from the bathroom floor; I did the same again in the hallway before returning to the bedroom and the bleakest of sights.

I had to change things. I didn't want Sarah being found in the state she was in. First, I cleaned her arms and wrists. With the towel, I removed the dried blood from her skin. Once she was clean, I took the razor blades out of my pocket and wrapped them up with the now dirty towel. I fetched a black bin bag from the kitchen and put the towel inside it. The bed sheet and the duvet were the next things I attended to. I pulled the duvet back from the bed and changed the cover for a fresh one from the linen cupboard. That was the easy part.

Then I had to change the bed sheet itself. But Sarah was immovable. I tried to lift her, but her body was now too heavy and rigid. I had to work around her. I started on my side of the bed and took the sheet off the mattress. I did the same again on Sarah's side before rolling her over slightly, which allowed the sheet to be removed freely. It turned out not to be too awkward, and I managed to reverse the procedure when I put the fresh sheet on. In the bin bag, I put the dirty sheet along with the other horrible artefacts.

Sarah now lay on a fresh-scented bed, still naked. I looked in the wardrobe for something to change her into. Her wedding dress was there, folded up in a box, but that didn't feel right or appropriate. Among lots of other dresses that hung in the cupboard, a long pink one stood out. It was her favourite; it was my favourite. She had only worn it on special occasions, and this was way beyond a special occasion. It had to be that dress, no doubt about it.

It took me a while to manoeuvre her into it. Eventually I succeeded. Even now, she still looked good in the dress – outstanding, actually. But her transformation wasn't complete. Her blue lips told the true story. I took out her make-up bags and juggled around with various lipsticks, testing them on the back of my hand. I had five stripes across my skin before I found a match on the sixth attempt. I covered her blue lips with pink, and took a step back. She was beautiful again. I covered her with the duvet and straightened everything up. All was now fresh and clean.

I felt the need to provide an explanation for what some poor person would find. I didn't want them to feel guilty or worried about anything. In the note, I explained what Sarah had done, and then wrote about my own feelings on finding her. I told them not to be sad; everything that followed from Sarah's death was necessary. The note wasn't long, but it said all that needed to be said. When I was happy with what I'd written, I put the letter in an envelope and placed it on the bed next to Sarah. Finally, I went to the living room, where I retrieved the present I'd bought for her. I unwrapped the photo frame and took it to the bedroom. I wanted whoever found Sarah to look at the picture and see how happy we'd been together. It was time for me to leave her, time to say goodbye to my love. I touched her face, got down on one knee and then held her left hand in both of mine, as if I were about to propose to her for a second time.

'I can't believe things have ended like this. I'm sorry for everything. I'm sorry for not being there enough. If only I'd read the signs properly, I could have stopped this from happening and we'd still be together. For that, I cannot forgive myself. You need to know that I love you, Sarah, and have never stopped loving you, not for one single second. And I will love you right up until the final moment of my life and beyond. Then maybe, when this is all over, we'll be together again on the other side. I'm so sorry. I love you.'

The tears started to flow again. I wiped them away with my sleeve before kissing Sarah on her cold, pink, stiffened lips. As I walked out of the room, I picked up the black bin bag that was sitting on the floor and left my wife for the final time, shutting the door behind me. Before I left the flat, I collected all that was needed for my big farewell. I went to the kitchen and armed myself with a bottle of vodka. I took the drawing that Sarah had done, along with the full bottle and the bin bag, and went outside.

I gladly dumped the bin bag in the wheelie bin and got

into the car. Most of its bodywork was hidden by a thick layer of snow. I turned the engine over, putting on the window wipers and clearing the snow off the front windscreen. Nerves were kicking in, so I opened the bottle of vodka and took the biggest gulp I could manage without throwing up. The taste was fiery. I could feel the clear liquid burning as it travelled down my oesophagus before hitting my hollow, starved stomach. That didn't put me off, though. I took three more gulps in quick succession. The final preparation was to place the drawing on the dashboard, so that it was visible at all times. With the open bottle secured between my thighs, I pressed my foot down on the accelerator, beginning my journey to the end.

I drove past places I'd been to with Sarah. I went by restaurants that we'd dined in, pubs and bars where we'd drunk, parks where we'd walked. Memories were crowding in on each other in my mind. I drove slowly and cautiously to avoid being pulled over by any passing police. When I drank the vodka, I made sure that I was in a secluded street and that the car was stationary. About halfway down the bottle, I began feeling drunk enough to know my handling of the car would suffer. It was now time for the final act. Time for the conclusion to my heartache.

I scoured the back streets of Corstorphine, looking for the perfect spot, and it wasn't long before I found the dead end I was looking for. It was a quiet, forgotten street – no people, not a sound – and at the end of it stood a solid ten-foot-high brick wall. My body was shaking, but that was due more to starvation and sleep deprivation than to nerves. Inside I felt calm and ready.

My foot revved the accelerator. I took the bottle of vodka, poured some of it over my head and drank what was left before setting the empty bottle down on the passenger seat. I retrieved the drawing from the dashboard, kissed it, folded it up and put it into the breast pocket of my jacket.

I started to drive with the accelerator pressed hard to the floor. The wall hurtled closer, growing bigger by the second. My heart was thumping. I had to press my foot down even harder on the pedal to stop my leg from shaking. I was now less than ten metres from the wall. I took my left hand off the steering wheel and unclipped my seat belt. The wall was right in front of me. My toes curled and clenched, both hands now gripping the steering wheel tightly. I swear I felt the impact before it actually happened.

The car hit the wall and I flew uncontrollably from the seat, my face meeting the windscreen. Eyes closed, I went head first into the wall. The force of the impact was immense, but it was painless.

# voices and the emergency room

Sirens and screaming filled the air. I could feel the cold metal of the car bonnet under my back, while my head was pressed up hard against the brick wall. My body felt twisted and uncomfortable. Bones were out of place. I tried to force my eyes open, but they wouldn't respond. I tried moving my arms, but they didn't work either. I couldn't even wiggle my toes. I could feel blood trickling from my ears, and the bitter cold stinging as it bit into a crack in my skull. A waterfall of blood was flowing from the wound, a constant stream of scarlet. Despite my condition, I was truly numb to any pain, for which I was thankful. I had hoped it would all be over as soon as I crashed into the wall. Instead, while I lay in my crooked position, I heard people talking nearby, and could make out the sound of women and children crying, horrified at the sight that met them in their quiet street.

The sirens stopped. I sensed people approaching me. I felt my body being slowly moved on to a stretcher, and then I was lifted from the wreckage. My neck was put in a brace. An oxygen mask was pressed to my face. The elastic strap stretched around the back of my head and tugged on my blood-soaked hair. I heard the ambulance doors closing, muffling the sounds of the sickened crowd. The sirens started up again and we began moving fast. I lay in the back of the ambulance, still and near-comatose. And then, quite clearly, I heard voices discussing me.

'I can't believe this guy's not dead already!' said a youngish female voice.

'Me neither, but I don't think he'll make it, not with a head wound like that,' replied a husky male voice.

'I wonder why he did it. What would possess someone to do something like that? I have to say, it was a horrible thing to see. I don't think I've ever seen a body so badly wrecked like that.'

'Well, you'd better get used to it, and quickly. You're only new, but you're going to see a lot more stuff like this on a regular basis. You'll see some sickening sights and never forget them … never. I still have nightmares about some of the things I've seen.'

There was a brief, thoughtful hiatus and then the female spoke again.

'He doesn't even look that old. He's near my age, I can tell. Why would he do that to himself? Why?' she asked, sounding genuinely upset.

'I don't know. Maybe if he pulls through you can ask him.'

'Let's hope he does.'

'I think we'll need to cross our fingers on that one.'

'I'm going to cross my fingers and my toes. I'm going to cross everything for him. I really hope he makes it.'

Their conversation ended. There was now only the

sound of sirens keeping me company as we made our way to the hospital. Every now and again I'd hear the driver of the ambulance shouting and swearing at ignorant drivers oblivious to the flashing lights and the high-pitched screams from the sirens. The drive didn't take long. Once the ambulance stopped I heard a rush of people. The stretcher I was spread across was being moved around at lightning speed. For a split second I felt the cold air again, and then warmth as I was taken straight into the hospital. Voices spoke, sharp and serious. Words like 'trauma' and 'operate' were used, and then I heard someone say 'life support'.

After the rush of being transported to the emergency unit, everything was still again. Then there was the sound of scissors being used, and I felt the clothes being cut from my broken body. They were heavy, drenched with blood. The further I was stripped, the lighter I felt. A weight was being lifted from me.

Tubes were inserted into my mouth. They were manoeuvred and forced down my throat. Needles were jabbed into my skin, into my veins, and some sort of liquid was injected into me. I was hooked up to all sorts of machines. I felt more uncomfortable than ever before. I wished they'd left me the way I was, against the wall, bleeding to death.

As parts of me were being tugged and pulled on, the voices started up again. They spoke over the sound of escalating beeps from the life-support equipment.

'We've got to do it now ... we've got to operate! We're running out of time. If we don't do it, we're going to lose him,' said one of the voices.

Hearing that, I felt an intense jolt of energy run through my body. Maybe it was the drugs that they'd just injected. Whatever it was, I felt awake again. My eyes clicked open almost instantly.

'His eyes ... his eyes are open!' said a female voice.

It was the same voice that had accompanied me in the ambulance, the young, timid voice. I couldn't move my head, but I moved my eyes and looked at the woman. Despite the tubes down my throat, I managed to speak.

'Come close,' I said to her.

She looked towards a few of the other people in the room, the surgeons and doctors, and they all waved her forward. She seemed nervous about putting her head close to my face.

'What is it?' she asked.

'I want to die. Please don't save me ... please let me die. I need to leave this place. There's nothing here for me anymore,' I told her.

She looked shocked, and I felt sorry for burdening her with such a serious request. She retreated from me, taking up her previous position next to the other hospital staff.

There was a momentary pause, and then one of the surgeons asked her what I'd said. Her response was a lie. She told them that she couldn't make it out, that it was just a meaningless mumble, a blood-bubbled garble.

Only I knew she was lying. The look of disbelief on her face when I'd told her I wanted to die indicated that she'd understood my request only too well. But I could understand her impulse to lie about it too. I could understand her fear. They continued with their plans to save me, but I had plans of my own. I closed my eyes. Before I shut my mouth for the final time, I took one last deep breath and held it.

This breath would be my last in the living world, I vowed. I held on to it tightly, refusing to take in more air. I felt my heart racing. I could feel it squirming and tightening inside my chest. This was the conclusion to my life. I heard the heart monitor picking up speed, and at one point it was hard to hear any intervals between the beeps. When my heart understood the situation it unclenched and the beeping slowed radically. I heard panic and urgency in the voices all around me. I even heard the young woman from the ambulance spill out the truth to her colleagues. Although the response she received from them was ignorant and throwaway, her honesty pleased me. It showed real courage and care.

Eventually the beeping stopped. The noise turned into a flat tone that continued for half a minute. While I waited to die, I felt my chest and body bouncing up and down as someone tried resuscitating me with a defibrillator. But no amount of electric shocks could bring me back. I didn't have the will to live anymore, and my heart and my head realised that. After a few failed attempts, the emergency team gave up. It was over. My body was still. The machines had been switched off. My head spun like a whirlwind. It felt like it was caving in on itself. I felt dizzy and nauseous; then something finally snapped and that was it. Everything turned black. The light of my life had been switched off. I was relieved.

# the finale

After I'd spent an indeterminate time in the darkness of death, a light was turned on. I was no longer in the hospital. I was in the white world of my dreams. I stood naked and alone. I took hesitant steps, looking all around me. There was nothing visible – just white, white, and more white. If this was heaven then it wasn't very interesting, I thought to myself as I circled back to my original position … then I nearly died again.

She was there; they both were, not too far away. She was wearing that dress, the pink one I'd chosen for her at the end. She looked radiant and glowing. Her face had a natural colour. It was beaming. From where I stood, I could see her smile. The most important thing, though, was what she held in her arms. It was our baby James and she was rocking him back and forth. He was dressed in a white bodysuit. I couldn't see his face but I caught a glimpse of movement, an arm dangling in the air, and nearly collapsed with joy. I'd never felt such exhilaration and love as I did in that moment. My broken heart instantly mended. It was pulsating rapidly with excitement. I wanted to run to them both and hold them, but something stopped me from doing so. Maybe I was supposed to savour everything about this remarkable situation I found myself lost in.

I took my first steps towards them and something strange, unexpected and otherworldly happened. There was a grumbling sound, as if the white world was hungry. That was quickly followed by a loud growl, then an ear-splitting roar. The sound was similar to that of a thunderstorm, but the noise was coming from under the white surface. It vibrated like an earthquake, shaking us all. It caught me off guard and I lost my footing and fell to my knees. Before getting back to my feet, I looked at Sarah. My first thought was to make sure that she and James were unaffected. Despite a slight loss of balance, she remained standing, a smile of pure happiness on her face.

Once the vibrations had settled and then stopped, I got back on my feet. Sarah lifted her arm and pointed at me. At first I wasn't sure what she was pointing at, but as I took my second step towards her I saw what it was. There was now a trouser leg visible rather than my bare flesh. I stood still and investigated the rest of my body. I was suited and booted. It was the same suit I'd worn when I crashed the car on my final day. It was my death suit, now in pristine condition. It had never looked smarter or fitted so well.

I started to walk again and straight away the scenery around me changed. I felt the surface beneath my polished black shoes turn springy. A small section of the white ground had greened over with fresh grass accompanied by its familiar summery fragrance. I lifted my head to look at Sarah and saw the greenness spread across the whole expanse of white between us. I watched as it neared Sarah and James, and she gleefully allowed it to sweep under her feet. And there it was: all the featureless white ground was now completely green.

I knelt down and felt the grass. With both hands, I gripped clumps of it tightly. Blades of green poked out through the gaps between my fingers. It was real. I stood again and dusted down the knees of my trousers, removing the grass that had stuck to them. Now I knew what to expect. Each step that I took would be met with an extraordinary happening. I tried to prepare myself for the next one, the next step, and took it gradually. As I lifted my foot from the ground, the roars and growls began again, but this time they were even louder and more unnerving. I threw myself to the ground voluntarily, in anticipation of being forced to do so by the quaking, shaking ground. On my hands and knees, I caught sight of Sarah. Somehow she remained standing. Between us, a section of the ground began to crack open and blades of the newly formed grass broke free from the earth and flew up into the air. There was now a large hole in the ground.

From it grew a gigantic oak tree. It stretched high into the pale sky, and then it came alive. The branches moved like arms. They lifted outwards in different directions, different angles. Once the tree had settled itself, the movement stopped. The hole that it had come from closed up, sealing itself around the trunk. Now the leaves came to life.

One by one they lifted themselves. Instead of lying inert on the branches, they began to express themselves. They stood up, tips pointing outwards. They were like an army of leaves, a paradoxically friendly army, dressed in the uniform of love. Then, like the tree, they settled, and all movement stopped. I waited for something more to happen, but it didn't. I watched the leaves, but in the windless setting they didn't move. They were perfect. When I got to my feet once more, Sarah was out of sight. Anxiously, I took a couple of sideways steps, and was relieved to see her and James again.

Now enough was enough. If things were going to happen, if things were going to change, then they may as well do so fast! My patience had been used up. All I wanted was to wrap my arms around my wife and son. I loosened my black tie before taking it off completely. This didn't seem like a black-tie occasion so I dropped it on the grass. I looked at Sarah before going to her, and we both smiled simultaneously. In slow motion, she blew me a kiss and signalled for me to come to her. So I did. I ran. All the different noises that had previously accompanied my movements were in full flow, but this time they didn't scare me. I embraced them. As I ran the short distance towards my family, I could see everything changing. Everywhere I looked, white was being replaced with different colours – the brightest hues imaginable being painted over the once-blank canvas.

Overhead was a blue sky. It was clear as water, with no

clouds. Swallows, robins and other birds were chirping and swooping through it. Some flew close to my head and others settled on the branches of the oak tree. Daffodils and dandelions, sunflowers and daisies, all spurted up through the grass, adding further bright splashes of colour. Rabbits roamed, hopping, ears flopping. The sun rose low in the sky, looking almost close enough to touch, like a giant orange.

As our surroundings continued to change, I reached Sarah and James. I threw my arms around them both and kissed my wife on her warm, living lips.

Our embrace lasted a long time. While I was holding them both, I noticed the background changing. More trees were breaking through from the grass. The empty white space was quickly turning into a glorious forest.

Beyond the trees soared green hills and mountains; waterfalls surged and streams were flowing. We both cried happy tears. Sarah had droplets trickling down her cheeks, and I wiped them away with the fingers of my left hand. When I touched her face her skin felt warm, unlike the last time that I'd felt it. After I'd wiped her tears away, she did the same for me. I took half a step back from her, but I didn't let go. I'd never let go of her ever again. My attention turned to James. What kind of miracle was this? He was moving. He was gurgling. There were bubbles of saliva coming out of his mouth and sliding down his chin. His arms and legs were swinging and kicking, and his eyes were open. They were the same colour as mine, hazel brown with a slight hint of green, and they were fixed on me. Gently, I stroked his thin, black, baby hair and he gave me a giggle and a gummy smile. I kissed him, and then I kissed Sarah again.

There were no words to describe the feelings that overcame me, no words to describe how happy I was. We were together again as a family. We'd yearned for this. Now it was ours.

I had to check one final thing. As Sarah held James in her left arm, I took hold of her right one and turned it over to inspect her wrist. There was no sign of a cut, no scar, no legacy of suicide. I ran my hand up and down the inside of her arm, from the wrist to the elbow joint, looking for broken skin, but the only thing I felt was her warm blood pulsing. She switched her holding of James and I carried out the same inspection on her left arm, with the same result. It was time for me to speak.

'Where are we?' I asked.

'I don't know, and I don't care. As long as we're together again, as a family, that's all I'm bothered about.'

'Me too,' I replied.

'It really is beautiful, isn't it?'

'It is. How long have you been here?' I asked her.

'I couldn't say. It's hard to judge time when everywhere you look is white. There was no night, no day.'

'Do you think we're alive?'

'No, I don't think so,' Sarah told me.

'Do you think this place could be heaven then?'

'I'm not sure. I don't know what this is, but I've been here before, I know that for certain.'

'When were you here?' I asked, surprised.

'After we'd lost James I started having strange dreams, dreams about this place, and every time I did he would be here. They felt real, very real. I started believing in them, and I believed in this place. I knew if I made it here, I would be with James again.'

'Is that why you left me? Is that why you did what you did?' I asked.

'Yes. It wasn't because I didn't love you. It was from a mixture of heartbreak and depression. The pills, the dreams, exhaustion. It was everything that had happened. I was drawn to this place instead.'

'I've been here too. I've had the same dreams,' I said excitedly.

'There was no other way for us to be with him. We had to come here. We didn't have a choice.'

'Well, I'm glad I came. I'm glad I joined you.'

'I love you,' said Sarah. 'I didn't tell you that enough, did I?'

'That's okay. I know you do. You don't have to tell me. And I love you too. I love you so much. And James. I love everything about him. I love having a family.'

'It's everything I ever wanted,' Sarah told me.

'I know. So ... what do we do now?' I asked.

'We walk.'

Sarah put one of her unscarred arms out in front of her,

pointing to a newly formed pathway that had appeared silently out of nowhere. The path stretched ahead for as far as my eyes could see. It went beyond the forest, into the hills and mountains, into the distance.

'What happens when it ends?' I asked my wife.

'We turn around and come back. We keep walking, together. And you never know, there could be more people like us somewhere along the way. We need to find them if there are. We need to walk.'

So that's what we did. I held on tight to my wife's hand and made a vow to myself that it would never leave mine again. I wanted to feel her with me forever. She held James in her other arm and we began our journey into the unknown, unlived world, one made especially for us. This was a new start. Although I had died, it felt like I had just been born again.

# acknowledgements

I would like to express my utmost gratitude to the following people: Gavin Marshall, Stuart Polson, Lynn Curtis, Elaine Sharples, and Louise Harnby. Without your input, patience, guidance, and overall hard work, this book would never have reached completion. You have all helped turn my little story into something I can be really proud of. I am so grateful for that. Thank you.

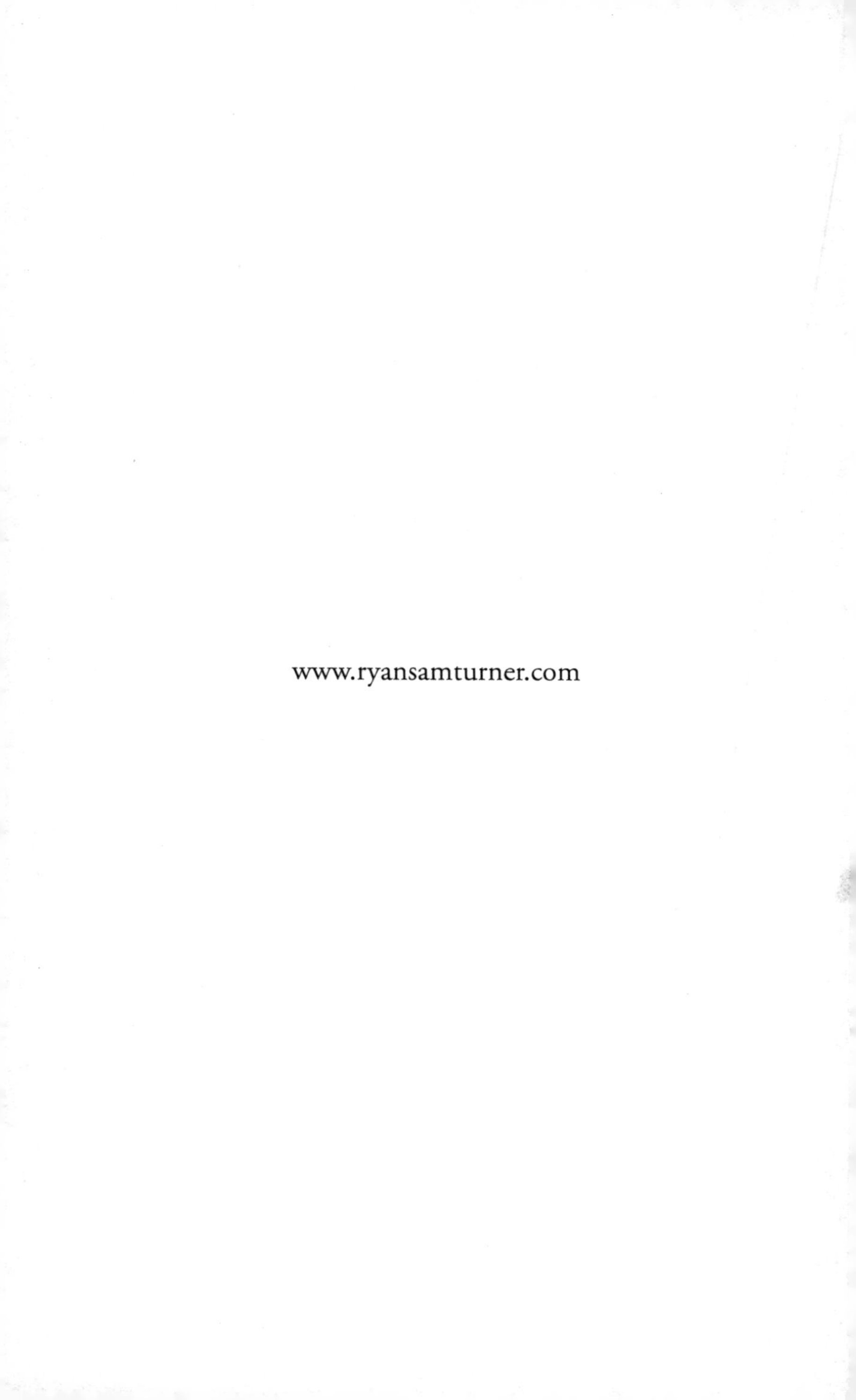

www.ryansamturner.com